The Guardians of the Sun-Star and Moon-Star

Book One

By

Sylvie Gionet

Certification Date July 2015–Present License 1123321 (Title) The Guardians of the Sun-Star and Moon-Star (Book I)

Canadian Intellectual Property Office-Certificates of Registration of Copyright Category-literary

Second Edition

Special thanks to Laurence O'Bryan and Tanja from BooksGoSocial

Edited by Jacqui Corn-Uys

Cover Design: Natasja from BooksGoSocial

ISBN: 978-0-9948553-3-6

Character Index

1) Earth: The Texas observatory, owner Dr. Knight

Project Solar Escape

Leading scientists: Gabrielle Gibbor and Michael Abba

The Orion constellation sent a leading light down to Earth

Michael and Gabrielle set out on a journey to find this light

Scientists on board at the Texas observatory:

Astrophysicists Betty Grant, Linda Stevens, Frank Connors, Josh Knight, and Sandra Collins

Cosmologist Jimmy Black

Astronomer George Snider

Associate to the Texas observatory

Archaeologist Blake Knight

Associates to the Texas observatory

Planetary Geologist Dean Briggs and Astro Meteorologist Zach Torn

2) Egyptian observatory: Scientist Ammon Daher

Orion constellation, Meissa

Lieutenant Johnson

General Clark

Taxi driver: Tadeas Almasi

Egypt, where a pyramid made of bronze and silver remained inside a vaporous cloud Inside was the Golden Door and a heavenly group of individuals

Metatron and Sandalphon

Temperance

Osahar and Mira

Pharaoh and a queen

Expert scientist Dr. Knight searched for Gabrielle in Egypt. He investigated a mysterious pyramid in Egypt alongside a group of his colleagues from the Texas observatory

Astrophysicists Sandra Collins

Cosmologist Jimmy Black

Astronomer George Snider

3) South African observatory: Scientist, Andricia Pillay. Searched for Michael in the Bakoni Ruins

The Orion Nebula connected to the Bakoni Ruins

The South African observatory linked up with the bronze and silver pyramid and the Golden Door

Brigadier General Dineo Davids, and Major General Azille Jansen

Raziel, bearer of the Fountain of Enlightenment

Hamuel

Nine scientists at a Space Agency

4) Italy observatory: Scientist, Marco Abelli, Pluto

Orion constellation, Mintaka

5) Canada observatory: Scientist, Liam Adams

Orion constellation, Rigel

Raphael

Set of connections, Mercury, and a duplicate in the new solar system

6) Turkey observatory: Scientist, Adlet Sezer

Orion constellation, Alnitak

Set of connections, Jupiter, and a duplicate in the new solar system

7) China observatory: Scientist, Bing Cheng

Orion constellation, Alnilam

Set of connections, Saturn, and a duplicate in the new solar system

Cassiel, bearer of the Tree of Life

8) Australia observatory: Scientist, Jacob Jones

Orion constellation, Sigma Orionis

Set of connections, Uranus, and a duplicate in the new solar system.

Raguelle

9) Mexico observatory: Scientist, Juan Beltre

Orion constellation, Betelgeuse

Set of connections, Neptune, and a duplicate in the new solar system

Saffron

Efren

Sariel

10) England observatory: Scientist, Angela Jones

Orion constellation, Bellatrix

Set of connections, Venus, and a duplicate in the new solar system

Anaelle

11) Austria observatory: Scientist, Adalard Dorn

Orion constellation, Saiph

Set of connections, Mars, and a duplicate in the new solar system

Northern side of the new planet

Gabrielle Gibbor

Moon-Star

The High Priestess

Saffron

Female army

Followers

Wizards Valda and Vance

Queen of Scepters

Silver gate, queen

Northern and Southern side of the new planet

Ariel, sacred native spirit animals

Uriel

Southern side of the new planet

Michael Abba

Sun-Star

Efren

Male army

Followers

Bronze gate, pharaoh

Dante, Four of Pentacles, six chalices

Heavenly leader, Paul, and his family

Grand Temple

Eastern side of the new planet

Josh and Blake Knight

Cassiel

Celestial warriors

Followers

Western side of the new planet

Sandalphon

Bronze serpent

Two dark entities

Contents

Chapter One
Michael and Gabrielle's First Vision

Are we alone or are we a replicated world, power-driven by the gods in the vast universe?

It was a normal workday for the team of astrophysicists at the large Texas observatory where our story unfolds. In the Department of Astronomy and Astrophysics, scientists' studies branched out far in the universe. Dr. Ben Knight is the owner and head of the Texas observatory. Researching everything that has had a lasting impact on creation is his goal. When Dr. Knight was absent from the observatory, he instructed the scientists to forward their data results to nine leading scientists at a Space Agency.

Gabrielle Gibbor is one of the observatory's employees. She soon became one of Ben's primary team leaders one year after Josh Knight, Michael Abba, and Sandra Collins came on board.

Gabrielle works alongside Michael Abba, and his biggest desire is to find that eccentric stellar entity in the cosmos. He wants to be the one who makes the biggest cosmological discovery of this century.

The observatory has a direct connection with leading scientists from around the world who collaborate with Ben's team to share their findings. Today's technology could reveal what has existed for billions of years in the universe. The teams make use of a variety of complex approaches to decipher the unusual phenomenon. When their focus shifted to the universe's outer limits, the scientists noticed substantial changes. It was apparent that a presence was about to alter the course of history.

It involved eleven observatories from around the world in what they had named Project Solar Escape. Any information or data regarding things that roamed in outer space or that sparked uncommon activity went to these scientists and the world's armed forces. The countries taking part were the US, Egypt, South Africa, Italy, Canada, England, Austria, Turkey, China, Australia, and Mexico. They became the earth's watchful eyes to study the puzzling changes in the universe. Whatever might unfold would require caution.

On March 20, 2015, a rare celestial alignment known as a trifecta was present in the cosmos. This had brought forth a full moon, a solar eclipse, and a spring equinox, otherwise known as the power of three. Because of the intense light emanating from the moon, it obscured the sun. They would create a great deal of future history for the ethereal realms together.

It is now April 20, 2015.

Over the last month, a vast number of extreme and irregular solar storms occurred, and from the perspective of planetary geologist Dean Briggs, Ben had learned, "There are strange changes taking place in the atmospheric environment. The atmosphere and the planet's geological history are changing, and an unusual transformation is happening at a rapid and troubling pace."

Astro meteorologist Zack Torn mentioned to Ben that he was keeping a close eye on this new transformation. The changes were speeding up. Observatories and scientists across the globe had determined that the climate was changing in a variety of alarming ways. No scientist could pinpoint what caused these changes. Nor could they determine the impact this would have on Earth and its ability to continue to sustain life.

***

The long night shift had ended, and along with it, twelve hours of stargazing. The night staff had finished recording the information they collected through the night and had prepared the data sheets for the day shift.

Gabrielle arrived early and parked her white sport utility F150 in front of the building. She was excited today as she had a surprise for the team at the observatory—she had cooked breakfast for them all! She stepped out of the truck and tossed her handbag over her shoulder. A bouquet of fresh flowers on the front seat had tuscan teal dahlias, daisies, and a few miniature sunflowers.

When she picked up the bouquet, Gabrielle looked up and noticed a beam of light shining through a low-lying cloud; it touched her and disappeared. Her eyes sparkled when she raised the bouquet up to her nose and waved the flowers back and forth as she took a sniff. The fragrance caused her to break into a smile. Making her way to the back of her vehicle, she flipped the tailgate down and placed her flowers on the bed liner. She

2

reached in and took out a large hamper packed with delicious food for the staff.

Armed with the hamper and flowers, she headed toward the lunchroom and placed them on a large wooden table. Shuffling through the hamper, she pulled out plates, forks, knives, and napkins and placed them on one end of the table. Moving back over to the hamper, she revealed the food and organized it on the other end of the table. Breakfast wraps, fruit salad, lemon, blueberry, and raspberry scones, and more. She then filled a vase with the flowers from her bouquet and the aroma of the hot food mingled with the sweet scent of the flowers.

***

Meanwhile, outside, Michael had pulled up to the observatory in his black sport, F150, but waited in his truck as he listened to an early morning talk show. He glanced at his watch, knowing that he needed to get into work. After getting out of the vehicle, he went inside and straight to the washroom.

***

Inside the observatory, Gabrielle bumped into Frank Connors strolling by the lunchroom. Frank had just got off the night shift. She approached him and said, in her usual offhand manner, "I brought food. Tell the rest of the staff. I know we all work long hours, so go eat breakfast before you head home."

"*Aw*, Gabrielle, thank you." Frank smiled at her; his tired eyes circled by dark rings. "You just saved me from stopping at one of those fast-food joints." Frank wandered off muttering about how he enjoyed having Gabrielle on his team, even if he only got to see her for a fleeting moment before he clocked out and went home to sleep. Frank then met up with Linda Stevens and Jimmy Black from the night shift, as well as Betty Grant and George Snider from the day shift.

"Gabrielle is at it again. She brought in her French cooking."

They all smiled in appreciation and headed for the food.

Soon Josh Knight popped in on his day off. He saw Gabrielle leaving the lunchroom, and he made his way over to see what she had brought in for breakfast.

***

As Michael exited the washroom, he clasped his hands together and his smile showed his mood. He headed over to the side entrance where their lab coats were hanging, slipped on his own lab coat, and buttoned it shut, ready to take on the day. But coffee first! He walked over to the coffee machine, poured water into the holder, and opened two large packages of coffee. After flipping the switch, he brewed a pot of strong coffee.

***

Frank had a deep, grateful smile when he met up with Gabrielle by the front door at the lab coat rack. He had made up a plate of food and was ready to go home. She walked by and smiled back at him. "Enjoy," she said while she put on her lab coat.

Sandra Collins approached her when she entered the command center. "Here are the data sheets from last evening."

Gabrielle looked up, startled. Today Sandra dressed to the hilt, and the smell of her perfume was overpowering. Sandra had caked her makeup on. Gabrielle wondered if she could get those lips any redder. Glancing down, she noticed Sandra wearing new stilettos and the question for a moment crossed her mind about who Sandra was trying to impress today. "Thank you, Sandra." Gabrielle tossed her a fake smile and walked away.

***

Michael wandered over to his computer and, with a push of a button, he brought up two sky maps on his screen. He could now see what had transpired in the night sky. Hearing footsteps, he turned his head and noticed Gabrielle holding a cup of coffee, strolling along, and reading at the same time. She caught his full attention. He stared at her and realized that this woman had become the best part of his workday. He took a deep breath and smiled.

"Good morning, Gabrielle." He almost sang her name out, but Gabrielle did not even seem to notice.

Gabrielle moved closer to Michael and continued studying the previous night's data analysis. "Morning, Michael. It looks like it is going to be an interesting day today. What do you think?"

In their busy part of the observatory, Gabrielle and Michael perceived things no one else seemed to notice. They both could see and feel transformations taking place in the cosmos that even the best-trained astrophysicists were not aware of. Gabrielle had considerable expertise in her field. As her talents stretched far beyond astrophysics, she could only appreciate her unique insights into these findings.

Michael glanced at the sky map, then turned and looked at Gabrielle. "Ah, something big is going on here. But I can't figure out what it is. Maybe we should examine this further."

Gabrielle stood by the computer and flipped the images across the screen. She reviewed the data that the scientists on the night shift had collected and stored over the past twelve hours.

"Yes. The solar system is shifting, and it is dramatic." She glanced at Michael, then back at the computer. "This isn't right."

They both moved into another area of the observatory, where George had brought up the latest information on a screen before heading off to collect his breakfast. Gabrielle hit a button and sent it over to their computers for review. All the staff worked together to study celestial objects and setup research on the current development. This was their primary focus. Gabrielle studied the findings George had brought up. She and Michael would have to make sense of them before they presented them to the world's nine leading scientists in a live conference call close to the end of their shift.

It was early morning, and she took her first sip of coffee, then she coughed. "Jeez! This is strong! Who made this coffee?" She turned and raised her cup with a bitter expression on her face.

"*Mm.* I did," Michael said. "Sorry." He scratched his head. *That was not the impression I wanted to make!*

She rolled her eyes, and they both laughed.

Michael was the joker in the observatory and kept everyone's spirits up. Not only did he have an eye for detail in all he did, but also had a farseeing gift and a powerful sixth sense. He forgot his embarrassment for a moment and gazed at Gabrielle, but she had already returned her thoughts to her computer and the sky map. She tucked her long, dark hair behind her ear as her hazel eyes scanned the screen.

Michael saw the rest of the night shift coming out of the lunchroom, carrying plates loaded with food. They headed toward the elevated seating area at the edge of the lab.

He leaned over and asked Gabrielle, "Did you bring food in again?"

She smiled and said, "Yes, Michael, go help yourself. I seem to be bored at night, which is why I started cooking and baking so often."

Michael perked up. This was the perfect opportunity to see if she wanted to go stargazing with him this evening. *I will wait until later, though, when there aren't so many people around.*

Turning his attention toward the lunchroom, he darted in and grabbed a plate, when he looked up and bumped into a wall. It was Josh towering over him; he had appeared out of nowhere.

"Wow, Josh, what are you doing here on your day off?"

"Last night I saw Gabrielle at the grocery store, and she mentioned she was bringing breakfast into work," Josh said through a grin. "I didn't want to miss out on that, so I thought I would join you guys."

Michael felt a pang of jealousy run through him. *I'm closer to her, seeing as we are both the observatory's primary team leaders. But Josh is Ben's son.*

"Wow, this food looks amazing, and she made those scones again. Look at the breakfast wraps, fruit salad, yummy crepes, and maple syrup. Are you kidding me?" Michael piled a generous portion onto his plate.

Gabrielle then showed up to grab her fill. Michael looked at her and said, "Very nice, plenty of food. Did you stay up all night cooking and baking?" Hinting around about what else she might have been doing the previous night besides preparing the delicious meal.

Gabrielle gave Michael a scathing look. "It's called being organized, Michael. I know what I want to bring, and I plan it all out the evening before."

He glanced over at her, his mouth breaking into a wide grin. Stuffing a scone into his mouth, he swallowed and said, "It's delicious, Gabrielle. You're fabulous . . . I mean . . . you're a fabulous cook."

She smiled in response. "Well, thank you, Michael."

The staff all chimed in, "Delicious food, Gabrielle. Thank you."

She peeked out the door and waved her arm at them. "I love to cook, and you guys deserve it."

"These breakfast wraps are amazing. I can't stop eating them," Michael exclaimed.

As Michael noticed Josh standing there glaring at him, he thought, *I hope he leaves soon, so I can chat with her before she begins her work schedule.*

"Hey, Gabrielle," Josh said. "It was good to see you at the store last night—your grocery shopping paid off. So, this is exciting news you were speaking about. What is it?"

She walked over to Josh and greeted him, but ignored the question.

"Good morning, Josh."

"Thanks for inviting me for breakfast." Josh then winked at her.

She smiled back at him. "No problem, Josh. Anytime. It's nice of you to come in on your day off," she said through a puzzled expression, as though she did not know what he was talking about.

Michael frowned at the interaction between Josh and Gabrielle and put his plate down and left the lunchroom to head for his workspace. Before he walked out, he looked back at them once more.

Gabrielle looked at her watch and said, "Got to go, Josh. Enjoy your breakfast." And then turned and left. His mouth was full, and he didn't have time to say anything.

She headed back out and walked with Michael into the observatory. As she turned her attention to the sky map, she saw in the measurements this was not right. She asked Michael, "Is this an equipment malfunction?"

"I don't know," Michael replied. "It seems no one else is seeing it. Why is that?"

They both continued checking out the reports on the previous night's cosmic activity. This could be just another stellar flare. But was it?

Josh wandered into the observatory and then headed straight toward Gabrielle.

He leaned up against her and said, "Goodbye, Gabrielle, thanks for breakfast." He brushed his lips across her cheek.

Gabrielle turned and stared right into his green eyes. Now he had her attention.

Michael glared up at Josh and noticed his gesture had surprised her.

She leaned back on her computer desk and tightened her hands around the table edges. But Josh just stood in front of her and continued, "Blake and I are heading out on a four-day fishing trip."

She responded, "Well then, you're welcome, and have an exciting time. I hope you catch lots of fish. And no problem with the food; I made it for everyone."

He leaned near her and whispered, "I guess we should have a fish fry when I get back? We can talk about what you said last night."

Gabrielle glared at him but did not respond.

It seemed to Michael she also had a hint of confusion on her face. Josh was just winding her up.

Josh nodded at Michael. "See you later," he said.

"Sure thing, Josh. Say hello to Blake and have fun fishing," Michael replied.

Josh winked at Gabrielle and left the observatory.

What's going on between those two? Just thinking about Josh getting to Gabrielle before him made him feel a little down. He decided he was going to be a gentleman, however. Michael never mixed work and pleasure. Besides, Gabrielle was not about to become somebody's trophy girl. Michael respected her and had given it time; to wait and see whether she could ever be interested in him. So, he gave her the chance to make the first move. Now he was wondering if he made the right decision. Josh appeared as though he was moving in on her.

Michael would take his time and figure it out from there.

***

Several scientists from around the world took part in Project Solar Escape run by Dr. Ben Knight. As the morning progressed, they relayed information about their observations from the previous night's activities out in the universe.

Ben's team of astrophysicists had observed a great deal of brightness around Orion's Belt, and the surrounding constellations in Orion were flaring. They resembled clusters of glittering diamonds in the dark universe. The other scientists' work kept them all busy, but they were oblivious to this current transition that was taking place in the universe.

Michael and Gabrielle were busy sending out the analyzed data to the adjoining countries to see whether they could make anything of last night's activity. However, this vision from the night before seemed to be for Gabrielle's and Michael's eyes only.

Then bang! As they looked up, there were multiple beams of light emanating from the outer planets in the earth's solar system. Just hovering there. The bright lights shone and glowed everywhere, their rays cast outward and into the vast universe.

Gabrielle and Michael turned and stared at each other; their faces were expressions of wonder and awe. No words could escape them as they tried to take it all in.

Gabrielle was the first to speak. "What's going on here? The solar system is acting odd. What do you think is going on here, Michael?"

He shrugged, then turned his attention to the recorded information on the sky map and studied it.

Gabrielle stepped closer and asked him, "Where are all these beams of light coming from?"

They both moved away from the sky map and glanced around the observatory. Everyone else was just carrying on with their work like it was an ordinary day. No one noticed this strange phenomenon.

"Maybe it's just another solar flare," Michael said. "We should monitor it. Over time, I'm sure it'll return to normal."

They both continued to study these curious, dominant courses of light. Gabrielle stayed fascinated, yet Michael looked confused. They both had ideas about what this might be. However, little did they know it would be hours, even days, before they reached a conclusion.

Gabrielle sensed something was not right; the idea sent a chill through her. She looked around her and wondered if she was forgetting something. Then she turned back to her work, certain that she could figure it out.

It was time for her to speak to the team. "There will be a total lunar eclipse in two days. This will be a rare one and it will darken the sky for four hours." They all turned and looked at her.

Betty shrugged her shoulders. "The upcoming eclipse is all they have been talking about for the past two weeks, since this alignment is so rare for this time of the year."

"Sorry," Gabrielle replied. "I was just thinking about the blood moon. I've never seen one before."

She frowned in thought for a moment, then turned back to Michael. "We won't see a celestial alignment like this again, at least not in our lifetime." Gabrielle wanted to share this information so all the team members could bounce ideas off each other.

"Listen up, all. Lunar tetrads are a series of four consecutive total lunar eclipses. The first of three eclipses of the tetrad took place on April 15, 2014, October 8, 2014, and April 4, 2015. Besides the final total lunar eclipse occurring on September 28, 2015, this blood moon will also be a rare one. The new records in front of me show that this blood moon will appear sooner, and it will put on a magical display on the horizon."

Michael's mouth formed into a slight smile. He crossed his arms and listened to her.

"During these phases, there will also be another remarkable event. The data shows that there will be a crescent moon on the evenings of June 19, 20, and 21, and Venus and Jupiter will line up, looking brilliant in the night sky. On June 30, Jupiter and Venus will align with each other. The stars will be one-third apart, creating a magnificent double star looking to the west; Regulus will shine alongside them. Last seen two thousand years ago, they say this star represents the star of Bethlehem. Still, all these phases are moving in fast and will occur at an earlier date in time."

"I am setting up the data sheets for the eclipse, Gabrielle," Sandra said. "We now have an idea when this is going to take place—thanks for the information."

Gabrielle glanced over at her. "You're welcome, Sandra."

Michael and Gabrielle both returned to studying the extraordinary event that was unfolding before them. Then they looked at each other as if realizing something, before returning their focus to the sky map. Orion's Belt had a shimmering look that was almost mesmerizing, and Gabrielle was sure they were falling under a spell. The Orion Nebula sent a signal along a narrow path into an area in South Africa, right on top of the Bakoni Ruins. This phenomenon showed up on their computer, but none of the other scientists were aware of it.

Another strange occurrence revealed that Meissa in Orion was sending a beam of light toward Egypt's Great Pyramids of Giza.

Gabrielle looked around the observatory, then leaned toward Michael and spoke in a faint voice, "Are we the only ones who can see this?" They both stepped back and took a breath.

Then Michael turned to the team. "Is anyone seeing anything unusual on the satellite or telescope recordings from yesterday evening?"

George, who was sitting next to Sandra, glanced at his screen, then turned to Michael. "Not too much activity, from what I can see. Everything appears normal here. I'm waiting for Betty's coordinates."

Betty chimed in, "Before I can give you an answer, or any coordinates. I need time to study the physics and math to see if there are any changes."

Sandra stepped away from her computer. "Is there anything I can help you with, Michael?"

"No thanks, Sandra. Gabrielle and I will take care of it."

Gabrielle stepped in front of Michael and blocked Sandra's view. "What do you think, Michael? Maybe we should investigate these areas."

A strange feeling came over her. She let out a breath and crossed her arms. "What is happening out there? We need to know what it is," she whispered.

"You bet. This looks important," Michael replied. "I don't understand why no one else thinks so. However, perhaps this is an opportunity to unveil a new discovery."

Gabrielle gazed around, then leaned toward Michael. "We should keep this quiet for now."

Michael winked at her. "No problem. I'm all in."

Her face lit up when she gazed back at him. "Well then, what do you think? Let's do it."

"Let's do what?" Michael pondered for a moment, then said, "No, you're kidding me."

"Why not? I'm the boss while Ben's away," Gabrielle said. "I've got the budget, and we both have the expertise."

They were both eager and excited that they may have decoded an unusual sighting in the universe. What was even more surprising was that none of the other scientists could see this phenomenon. They all used the same telescopes and studied the same satellite images.

"Alright, team. You are going to be on your own until Ben gets back. Gabrielle and I both have business to take care of," Michael announced.

Ben was away on business, and he had left Gabrielle and Michael in command of the observatory. The two discussed tactics and decided who would go where. They agreed she would go to the Great Pyramids of Giza, in Egypt, and he would go to the Bakoni Ruins in South Africa. Gabrielle penned a message for Ben, giving him a full description of what they had both observed, then she placed it on his desk and walked away.

Having overheard a bit of their conversation, Sandra moved toward Ben's desk. She picked up the note and took it back to her own desk to read. Then she flipped open her phone and texted Ben, all the while watching to see how close Gabrielle was standing to Michael.

With their plans made, Michael and Gabrielle headed out to the supply room on the bottom floor of the observatory. They each picked up a camera, video recorder, a laptop, tracking device, geothermal reader, and a few miscellaneous items, and packed them into duffel bags.

Before they headed off, Michael said to her, "Oops! We have packed our gear but forgotten about flights! Would you mind booking them? You know how bad I am at connections."

"Oh, Michael. If I didn't know you better, I'd say you were just trying to get out of it!" Gabrielle responded with a wink. "Plug your phone into this computer. I did a screenshot for our locations." When Gabrielle booted it up, they both plugged in their phones and Michael downloaded her screenshot. This download contained a detailed data analysis on these lights pointing in each direction.

As they walked out of the observatory, they stopped and stared at each other. A strange feeling had swept over Gabrielle, and she could see in Michael's eyes he felt it, too. A harmonizing love centered, it set in and made them aware of what one's role was in the world. They broke eye contact, and he took the duffel bags and put them in the back of his truck. With an excited glance at each other, they said goodbye, jumped into their trucks, and were off to their homes to pack whatever else they needed.

***

Gabrielle arrived at her home, opened the door, and threw her keys on the table. Then she rushed around the house and packed her luggage with the clothing and other necessities she would need for Egypt's tropical desert climate.

She walked over to the computer to boot it up and logged onto a couple of websites to compare flight prices. The cost of their return flights was $12,000 each. She usually planned these types of trips months in advance. How would she explain this one to Ben? She noticed her phone flashing a red indicator light, then it stopped. She figured it was her battery running low. Gabrielle plugged it in for a quick charge, then contacted the bank to have a considerable sum of money released; both she and Michael would need money for accommodation and other necessities.

Once done, she made the reservations then texted Michael their flight information, ending with: We're all set!

Michael returned her texts: You're outstanding, Gabrielle. I'm on my way. See you in ten.

She read the message, then called him instead of texting back. "I'm as ready as I can be, Michael."

He took a deep breath. "Excellent. We can get food at the airport. Sound good to you?"

She laughed and fired back at him, "Is eating all you do, Michael? I'll wait for you outside." She hung up, shoved her cell phone into her purse, grabbed her suitcase, locked the door behind her, and strolled outside.

Not long after, Michael arrived at Gabrielle's home. She hurried to his truck, tossed her luggage in the back, jumped in, and greeted him with a big grin. "Let's do this."

He leaned toward her and winked. "Away we go."

***

As they approached the airport, Gabrielle said, "This whole thing is intriguing. And I can't believe we both just up and left the observatory when Ben had left us in command. I hope we have the right skill set for this."

"Don't worry. Ben knows he has the best scientists in the field on his team. We won't disappoint him; I just wish we were both going to the same location."

Gabrielle didn't acknowledge his words, a thoughtful expression on her face. "We did this with no hesitation, Michael. Funny, isn't it?"

Michael looked confused. "Yes, it's all rather mysterious, but I believe this is a positive move."

He aimed a look at her, and his hands gripped the steering wheel. "Who knows where this might lead?"

"I agree, Michael. What is going on here we know little about. And it could very well have a major impact on the planet or maybe even the universe."

When they arrived at the airport's main entrance, they realized it was busy. Michael circled the parking lot, looking for a place to park for the duration of their trip. He found a spot in long-term parking, pulled in, and cut the engine. He hesitated, and said, "We owe Dr. Knight big."

"We sure do. Let's find a discovery he will be proud of."

Gabrielle got out of the truck to get a trolley, and they loaded it up.

As they walked toward the terminal, with Michael pulling the trolley, he tilted his head and focused his attention on the woman beside him. He realized just how beautiful she was. Michael felt a stirring in him as he drew closer to her. He wondered if this was love. He also suspected Gabrielle was already thinking ahead of Egypt and his thoughts should be about South Africa. But Gabrielle didn't seem to notice his stare.

Once they had both checked in, Michael grabbed two sandwiches to eat from the food court and two drinks. He met Gabrielle, where she had found a comfortable seating area. He sat down, and in between eating, they talked about what had directed them to this point in their lives, and how they both had a love for cosmology.

With their drinks raised, Michael said, "Cheers, Gabrielle. I hope we both make a miraculous discovery." Their glasses clinked.

Gabrielle leaned back and crossed her legs. She took a sip of her drink and must have noticed Michael staring at her.

As a voice over the loudspeaker announced her flight was boarding, they got up and hugged. Then they wished each other the best of luck. Michael touched her soft arms, gazed into her eyes, and said, "If you sense any danger, promise me you will leave."

Gabrielle gazed at him with her bright hazel eyes. "I promise. But the same goes for you. Take care, Michael."

They both sensed the warmth growing between them. The intensity built, and a potent force of energy connected them to each other. Michael was, at that moment, sure he was in love with Gabrielle. His piercing eyes were watching her. And the sweet smell of her perfume drew him in closer. He slid his hands over her bare arms once more. He wanted to profess his love for her now, but he knew it was too soon.

Gabrielle wrapped her arms around his solid frame, bracing him. She kissed him. He pulled her closer and held her, feeling the warmth running within his body; her kiss was irresistible. Then she turned and left.

Michael stood back and took a deep breath. "Whoa, I wasn't expecting that." He watched her walk through the security gate until he could see her no more and then bought another drink as he waited to board his flight.

His thoughts continued to flicker between their mission and Gabrielle herself. His flight's departure broadcasted, and he was on his way.

***

In the meantime, Ben had received Sandra's text message and was aware of the events that were taking place at the observatory and about Gabrielle and Michael's sudden departure. Ben was a man with his mind on his work. He already knew the solar system was shifting. And he suspected his observatory's two brightest scientists may have deciphered an unusual phenomenon out in the cosmos and on the planet. This early morning surprise had Ben leaving Italy. His good friend Marco Abelli had a private plane, fueled and ready to take him back to Texas.

***

Ten hours later, Ben was back in the observatory. He stood in front of his computer and conducted a global video conference with the ten contributing countries and the Space Agency.

"Okay, team, and hello to all of you online. This is Dr. Ben Knight from the Texas observatory reporting about the latest information. Gabrielle and Michael are two of my finest, and they are now heading to Egypt and South Africa. They might have made a breakthrough in the universe. We haven't noticed it yet. I have great faith in these two, so let's follow their progress. We have no concrete information yet as the two have not reported in, and I do not expect any contact with them until tomorrow since they are both in flight."

He picked up the note and read it aloud for everyone to hear. "Hi, Ben. After studying the data results from last night, we noticed on the sky map that there is a strange shift in our solar system. Luminous lights shine everywhere, but only Michael and I can see them. This unusual solar activity appears more frequently, and it's beyond our solar system. There are prominent linear lights shining all the way through the stratosphere to Egypt and South Africa. We hope you understand why we had to go. Being out in the field, and our love for cosmology, are our passions. Please have faith in us. The total lunar eclipse takes place in two days or even earlier, this may bring answers. We will stay in touch, Gabrielle and Michael."

Ben headed to the boardroom and turned on a sky cam that had a direct link to a secret location and a direct connection to the leaders of the world's defense for paranormal activity.

He communicated this latest news using a private encryption and put the Space Agency and the military on high alert. The scientists could now move their studies toward Egypt and South Africa.

Ben realized what an important discovery Gabrielle and Michael had made. Trying to keep his excitement in check, he turned to his team. "All of our expertise is now being put to the test. I can't stress enough how important this is. We need to direct our attention to the abnormal paradox Gabrielle and Michael mentioned. And I need to know what else they have seen."

Chapter Two
Egypt and South Africa

Gabrielle hailed a taxi. The airport was busy. Swerving through traffic, the taxi driver made his way to her. He screeched to a stop at the curb and rolled down his window. "Get in."

She tossed her luggage and duffel bag in the trunk, slipped into the car, and they headed out of the airport. He glanced into the rear-view mirror and asked, "Where would you like to go, young lady?"

"I need to get to the Pyramids of Giza, please," Gabrielle responded.

As they drove to her destination, she took in the intriguing architecture of the buildings. Her journey had left her drained, but she also felt excited about what she might find. When they arrived, she reached into her purse and pulled out Egyptian pounds she had exchanged at the airport to pay the man.

He looked over at her. "Would you like a pickup, miss?"

"Can I have your number, please? Later this evening, I will need a ride to my hotel."

He handed her his card. "Okay, so you're going to haul all that luggage around with you?" he said and shrugged his shoulders. "Please, call me."

She glanced down at his card. "Thank you, Tadeas Almasi."

Exiting the taxi, she tucked his card into her pocket. She grabbed her luggage and equipment and continued to the pyramids.

Scanning around the area, she noticed a lot of tourists roaming around the ancient monuments. The sights and the atmosphere lifted her spirits as she continued to an empty area nearby.

She grabbed her cell phone to call Michael and a red light flashed. "Shoot, my battery is dead again. It can't be—I charged it. What is that red light?" She thought about it and checked to see if she had a voice message, but when she listened to it, she heard nothing but static in the background. So, she unzipped her duffel bag and tossed out her equipment, then found a quick charge battery pack and placed her cell phone on it. As she waited, she examined the expansive Great Pyramids of Giza before her. A misty cloud hovered over the site, then a dazzling light shone through the haze.

The cloud soon rose, and she saw the beam of light at last coming in from a constellation in Orion. Without realizing she was moving; she was soon standing in front of the largest pyramid she had ever seen. To her knowledge, there was no record of this in existence. As if by magic, she was the lone visitor at this amazing site, and she did not know how she got there.

"Well, this is extraordinary," she said with a gasp. "Where did this come from? Why isn't anyone else surveying this and taking pictures of this great wonder?"

She looked over and saw that no one had noticed this. Instead, they continued with their own business. "This is odd. I'm calling Michael." She picked up her phone, but it went to his voice mail. She knew he was on his flight, and she smiled as she listened to Michael's message.

'Howdy. If I am not stargazing, I am gazing at beautiful women. Tell me what you fancy, and I will get back to you. Ciao!'

She laughed and then left a message. "Oh, you're a character. You will not believe what I've just discovered. A magnificent pyramid. I'm not sure what to make of this, but no one else around here appears to have noticed it.

She felt a chill running through her body. "There is a connection between this amazing discovery and the cosmos. And it's connected to you and me, Michael. But what is it? And why?" Gabrielle lost her connection to Michael; she flipped her phone shut. She hoped her message would get through when he landed at the airport.

As she stood by the entrance, Gabrielle took out her electromagnetic radiation detector to see whether she could register readings, but nothing showed up. She reached out and slid her hand over the outer wall. She saw this pyramid was pure bronze and silver with glowing mystical imagery etched into its exterior.

"*Hmmm.* I hope my equipment isn't malfunctioning. Well, well, well, should I enter or not? Of course, I should! I didn't come all this way to be a chicken, now did I?"

Gabrielle walked straight in once she decided. Two shimmering beams of light touched her and drew her through the pyramid's bronze and silver doors. As she wandered down the bronze and silver corridor, gleaming lanterns guided her way. Vine-covered walls covered the interior, and flowers in different colors twisted through the stems. Faceless carvings of bizarre images materialized on the walls. As she walked, the vines moved along with her. More lanterns lit up, one by one, and she could smell perfumed oils. Gabrielle took a deep breath. She was calmer now, and a warmth enveloped her. She felt like she was walking on a cloud. The enchanting energy she felt from the new pyramid drew her further in. She was both fascinated and a little nervous.

***

Michael arrived at the Nelspruit MQP-Kruger Mpumalanga International Airport.

He was mentally and physically exhausted and excited, wondering whether he would find the answers. He exchanged his dollars to rands and exited the airport, and stood at the curb, looking for a taxi. When he saw one, he waved it over.

"Can you take me to Machadodorp, where the Bakoni Ruins are on the escarpment?"

"Sure thing, hop in."

Michael tossed his luggage into the trunk, he slid into the back seat, and he was on his way. Watching his surroundings, he pondered. *These taxi drivers are unpredictable over here—look at them. Racing around here like their hair is on fire.* He gripped the door handle as the driver sped away from the airport. Glancing out the window, Michael could see that he was now amid heavy traffic; he jostled from side to side as his taxi zigzagged around cars that were changing lanes in front of him.

After traveling on tarred roads, they reached a gravel road, and the car kicked up clouds of dust. Michael rubbed his eyes and coughed, then he rolled up his window. He bounced around as the car ran through potholes. He was relieved when they arrived at his destination.

Michael booted up his cell phone and scrolled through to review his coordinates for the two beams of light that they had downloaded on their phones before they left. When he clicked his phone shut, he dug into his pocket and pulled out a billfold. He ripped off a few bills and handed them to the driver. "Thank you."

The driver smiled and said, "Would you like a pickup?"

Michael thought about it for a moment. "I'll put your number on my cell phone. Is that okay? Later this evening, I will need a ride to my hotel."

The driver handed him a card. "Well, if you are sure you're going to lug that baggage on that long path to reach the escarpment of the Ruins," he said and shrugged his shoulders. "No problem, call me anytime."

Michael clutched the card in his hand, glanced down at it, turned, and said, "Thank you, Tadeas Almasi."

He tucked the card deep into his pocket, exited the car, and pulled out his luggage. Tadeas turned the car around and nodded his head. Michael waved and watched him speed off and disappear into the distance.

His walk on a long path brought him to an area where he could take in the magnificent view of the Bakoni Ruins. It filled this immense area with the astonishing sight of hundreds, or even thousands, of ancient Ruins. Something or someone buried these circular stones in the terrain. Since the dawn of time, the Ruins had existed and remained a mystery.

"Off to work I go."

When it was time to set up a workspace, he noticed the sky becoming dim, but continued. He started with his equipment. First, he setup his tripods, then his video recorders. He flipped a switch, putting them on auto, and recorded. Next, he setup his laptop, plugging it into his solar battery, powering it up, and opening a digital sky map. Rifling through his duffel bag, he found his high-powered camera, slipped the straps over a shoulder, and started photographing the Ruins. As he moved around the crumbled stone walls that surrounded the ancient structures, it drew his attention to a particular area.

He stepped toward it, curious. Michael had only read about this in textbooks and journals. Now, he was looking at it first-hand. Just as he entered a small enclosure, a mass moved across the sky, darkening it. Michael sniffed the air. He smelled smoke and recognized the odor of burning sweet wood.

He looked around but could detect no one. The atmosphere heightened his range of view and his senses. Looking skyward, he observed a steady flow of light reflecting on the horizon, and his eyes brightened. The brilliant lights shone down on an area within the Bakoni Ruins. The sheer number of Ruins made him feel overwhelmed.

Above the area, a dazzling multicolored aurora borealis shimmered all around it. Michael stared up at it in awe.

"Wow, this is fantastic. Look at that sky! I hope Gabrielle can see this."

He photographed the area and focused on the lit Ruins.

Then he pulled out his cell phone and called Gabrielle. However, he got her voice mail and not that for which he was hoping. "Hello, Gabrielle. I am just checking in. How are things at the Egyptian pyramids? Call me when you can. I want you to be careful. I found a tremendous energy source in one Ruin. The geothermal energy readings are hitting the top of the scales. This Ruin is bright and glowing."

An unexpected flash of light distracted him.

"One Ruin, in particular, appears to be the only active one." He looked around and then continued, "This is bizarre, and it's glowing."

He shook his phone, but all he could hear was static.

Michael hoped the message went through despite the interference. He trusted they would connect soon. "I sure would like to hear from her."

As he studied the digital sky map and looked at Orion's Belt, he noticed the constellations in Orion were sparkling and it was becoming more peculiar. This was not the Orion's Belt astrophysicists knew; in fact, the view was almost otherworldly.

Michael dictated his findings into his computer: "Orion's Belt is no longer lined up with the Great Pyramids of Giza. From what I can see, it appears to be shifting. It is pulsating with a vigorous energy, and it looks to be casting out small linear lines of light."

He stopped and thought for a moment. The light in front of him came from within the constellation of Orion, and it lined up with one Ruin. It also projected a beam of light toward Egypt, where Gabrielle was.

Michael noted the solar system was shifting, and the constellations in Orion exhibited an extraordinary brightness. He stood back and took in a huge breath. He then shifted his gaze from the sky to the Ruins and back again.

"This is extraordinary. This is unimaginable. The solar system is shifting! But why me? Why Gabrielle? What does this have to do with us?"

He pressed the screen on his cell phone and tried to call Gabrielle again, but there was no reception. He shook his phone and held it up to his ear, but all he heard was static. "I can't believe it. I can't get hold of her."

Chapter Three
Project Solar Escape

Project Solar Escape closed off to the world, with no incoming or outgoing calls. This project was now a top-secret military investigation and would remain so until they figured out why the beams were there and if they had brought any alien life with them.

The astrophysicists saw a great visual streaming down to the adjoining countries, and they were adding it to the leading scientist's sky maps. The bright lights cast down from Orion's Belt and the constellations in Orion had caught their attention. All the celestial alignments were right in front of them, and only those with access to the observatories' high-powered telescopes and satellite imagery could view them. The world's military forces and the paranormal defense units received briefings about the possibility of warfare with an unknown entity.

Ben and the representatives of participating countries could feel the buzz of excitement leading to the total lunar eclipse. Italy then asked for permission to speak to all, on live sky cam, and Ben connected all the countries to listen in; a secret society of nine primary scientists and the world's military leaders also listened in, in the background.

"Good evening, hello from Italy. Marco Abelli here. I am glad you are back at your observatory, Ben. What we are now seeing is beyond words, my friends. We all wish Gabrielle and Michael the best of luck. I have exciting news for you. Pluto is on our doorstep. So, it looks like we in Italy are the eyes of Pluto, my friends. Our team has a full visual of Pluto, and we can see a magnificent light-yellow, heart-shaped shadow upon its surface. Its moons look spectacular. Another thing, Ben, we can see a shimmering light beaming from Pluto toward Mintaka. Orion's Belt is sparking up interesting beams of light. Direct hits are leading down toward Egypt, in the area where your colleague is. Pluto and its moons Charon, Kerberos, Styx, Hydra, and Nix lie 4.67 billion miles away, and they're right here. How do you like that? This is astounding!"

"How magnificent, thank you, Marco," Ben replied. "We cannot see that from here, so you are our eyes on Pluto, Italy. We will all need to update each other, as all activity is crucial now."

George then announced, "Ben, another call is coming in from Egypt."

"Hello, my friends, Ammon Daher here. We have a bright light beaming down from the constellation of Orion. The signal comes from Meissa. This brightness is pointing nearby here somewhere. We're not sure of the location. We can't get a reading on that area, but we'll keep you posted."

The messages were now pouring in, and Ben was on full alert.

"Hello from England, it's Angela Jones here. We are seeing a white planet out in the cosmos. It's very faint. But we believe it may be Venus right above us. The constellations in Orion are lighting up the sky. We have a signal from Bellatrix and a connection, but we don't know where the beam is pointing, as we can't get a full reading either."

"Hello from Mexico. Juan Beltre here. Greetings, my friends. The Orion constellation is sending a signal from Betelgeuse to Neptune, and we can see two ghostly images floating around it. They both appear to be supernatural. It's unusual."

"Okay, we now have a supernatural connection," Ben said. "Which is a brand-new discovery. We have a great deal ahead of us, so we need to maintain our composure. This is a once-in-a-lifetime experience. However, it is mandatory that we do our best to keep our world as safe as we can. A strange entity is flying above us. Be sharp, my friends."

Ben's observatory screens then filled with people from the project wanting to give their feedback. He equipped his teams with specialized equipment so they could view the meteorological and astronomical phenomena unfolding right before their eyes.

"Team Texas is ready to report; we have results," Sandra announced.

"Please begin," Ben said.

"We found a warning sign here in Texas, Ben," Betty reported. "There are two beams of light coming from Lota Orionis. This signal is pointing down to a place in South Africa."

Another call then came in from South Africa. Andricia Pillay put in her report. "The Orion Nebula is sending out a signal; it is a streaming light.

It's pointing down at the Bakoni Ruins. We can't zero in on the location or get any kind of reading yet."

"On behalf of all of us, Ben, we believe that what we are seeing here, these scattered beams of light, are searching for their place," Sandra said. "They're getting ready for a connection. What do you think?"

Ben reflected on his two closest colleagues out in the field. Strange activity was apparent on the horizon. He wondered what it set in motion for Gabrielle and Michael. Were they in trouble? Should he get them out? Or were they in a suitable position to shed light on this mystery?

He had an idea. "Perhaps Michael and Gabrielle can see this. There are beams of light going their way. Keep trying to contact them. Check the company credit card for any charges—Gabrielle has one. If you find either of their trucks parked anywhere, have it towed back here. Maybe they left more clues; they know more about this than we do."

"Gabrielle and Michael are still out of range," George responded. "We have left them many messages and they haven't replied. I am checking the company credit card, and it has extensive amounts charged to it, Ben. Hotel accommodations, as well as a flight to Egypt and South Africa. Dallas/Fort Worth International Airport had logged Michael's license plate in long-term parking. I am calling a tow truck to have it towed and to pay the bill."

"Good news. At least we found a truck and know which airport they both flew out of. I am concerned about their well-being," Ben said. "Let's hope we hear from them soon. All we can do is to continue and hope for the best."

Chapter Four
A Mysterious Encounter

Gabrielle reached the end of the pyramid's entrance and met an astounding view; it was a massive golden door. She stopped, looked up, and scanned it from left to right. The design of the door allowed it to fit to perfection; it covered the entire back area of the magnificent pyramid. A radiance of light emanated from it. Gabrielle stood in wonder; she could not believe what she was seeing.

"This is breathtaking! Is this for real?"

She stepped closer and realized how incredible this discovery was. An electrifying chill moved through her body. She drew in a breath and said, "I wish Michael could see this."

With a great deal of excitement, Gabrielle got to work. She opened her duffel bag and unloaded her equipment. The golden door pulsed and radiated a brightness again. She grabbed her camera and snapped photographs. Then she reached out and touched the door. As she ran her palm over its golden surface, an incredible surge of energy ran through her, and she felt a warmth controlling her body. She gasped for air as the stimulation she felt kept rising, giving her strength and stamina, and incredible vitality.

Her arms felt unusually strong when she raised them. "Wow," was all she could stammer, and she removed her hand from the forceful pull. Intuition made her feel that the discovery's source was a supernatural power. She moved back to take more pictures, then she setup her video equipment. A quick flash of light startled her. The engraved sculpted images on the golden door took more coherent shapes. She moved back and watched this astounding event unfold. Transformations on the surface of the golden door were now spreading out in a continuous motion.

As she examined the golden door, she realized it reflected an image of outer space, and the more it radiated, the more it drew in cosmic energy from afar. Gabrielle believed this door was hard-wired into the universe, and she was witnessing what was transpiring out in the cosmos at this very moment.

The shapes swirled, twisted, and turned, then an image of an unknown solar system materialized on the golden door. Planets aligned in a perfect circle! She jumped up and yelled out, "This is sensational! But how?" As amazing as it was to witness this, she wondered how the golden door could broadcast images on its surface from out of the universe.

"*Hmmm*, the planets in our solar system travel in elliptical orbits, rather than in perfect circles, which is what I am seeing here. So, the distance in this solar system will not change. This is astonishing; what a discovery!"

As Gabrielle watched, it felt like she was in a dream. Within the changing images, a glorious sun and moon appeared and eclipsed. She continued to record the discovery.

"Orion's Belt is so bright it radiates. Now its constellation is sending an intense lambent light from Betelgeuse, and I have a perfect view! It's directing the source of this effulgent light, and it appears to be shifting from Earth's solar system. Earth's Neptune is sending a beam of light straight to the discovered Neptune. The discovered planets are indeed putting on a wondrous chain of events. Now there are two lights coming from Betelgeuse. Two shadowy images channel a way to the new blood moon."

Gabrielle looked shocked as her vision focused on the unusual mental image.

"I don't believe what I am seeing. There are two ghostly images floating around the new blood moon; they are ethereal entities. One is wearing ivory and the other black. I wonder what or who they are? If I weren't recording this, no one would believe me. They appear to be waiting for something; I wonder what it could be?"

She checked the positioning on the screen of her video camera. As she continued to stare at the images, she realized what she saw back at the observatory made sense now.

Gabrielle continued videotaping and took more photographs. She was getting the excitement she was looking for. But the two ghostly images were making her feel uneasy. She took a deep breath to remain calm. The new solar system on the golden door was in 3-D, but the surrounding illustrations were still not clear, and she couldn't quite tell what they were. Then she felt a chill. It was as if someone had opened a door and a cool breeze had drifted in.

"There is a presence around me." Gabrielle spoke into the camera's microphone as she continued recording. "There is a spiritual existence on this door. I can feel it. It's like a superior power or being. Now I am seeing the markings of dark energy or a supernatural effect that seems to flow up toward a large black cloud. Wait, Pluto just appeared with all its moons."

She continued to record her findings, as her hands shook and heart pounded. She tried to document the details of what she was seeing and feeling while the golden door continued to cast bright lights and dark images.

"I see a very mysterious gloom in the area surrounding Pluto. And flickering lights disseminating from the dwarf planet. Otherwise, I can't tell what is happening."

She realized she was not alone. She felt a presence, and it was lurking around her. Then she felt her own extraordinary energy building up from within. She glanced to the right and then to the left. Then she turned around. She watched two shadowy figures floating toward her. A gloomy haze hung between them as they approached. She dropped her video recorder, backed away from the golden door, and trembled.

"What do you want?" She retreated from the two ghostly figures.

One figure answered, and his voice echoed off the metal interior, piercing her ears. "We are here to fulfill a prophecy; the time has come."

She spoke, asking in a nervous voice, "What kind of prophecy? Why are you here?" She thought about the rare total lunar eclipse that was now taking place and wondered if this could be a portent of what was to come. But Gabrielle had not heard of any prophecy. She thought the lunar eclipse was because of an unscheduled, onetime cosmic event.

Gabrielle felt unsettled. The two eerie, murky, cloaked figures landed in front of the golden door and stood there in silence. Then an enormous flash of light startled her and the dense smog surrounding the two darkened figures swirled. The ground vibrated, accompanied by a loud rumbling. The smog drifted to the floor and toward the golden door. Then the room oscillated, and a great wind blew in, whirling the coarse sand that flew everywhere. Gabrielle backed up and braced herself up against the pyramid's wall. She felt two handles and peeked down at them; she knew to hang onto them.

Even though things were spinning all over, she didn't want to cover her eyes. A noise was coming from the golden door, which sent chills through her body and a horrible smell like fresh blood seeped forth. She wanted to be a witness to what was taking place; she wanted to see and record it all. The active solar system on the golden door flashed. Pluto caught on fire, lighting up the sky, and the adjoining moon's appearance seemed erratic since they were all wobbling. The two cloaked images went up to the door. In an instant, a beam of light had transferred them both to the image of Pluto. The dark mist in the room overshadowed the golden door, then shrunk and established itself in the top left corner. Gabrielle became overwhelmed by what she had just witnessed. An invisible source of power had moved two resilient supernatural entities onto the golden door and straight up to Pluto. Gabrielle shivered.

"What just happened? This can't be good." She sighed and looked around her. The dark figures were gone, and the golden door reflected what she knew had already transpired in the universe. "All right, I need to calm down. I hope these abnormal events are over. I promised Michael that if I felt I was in danger, I would leave."

She rummaged through her duffel bag and pulled out her thermos. She took a drink of water and did her best to push back her fear. These unexpected events in the pyramid had her worried, and she wondered if she could even leave. However, she knew she would not give up studying this discovery for anything.

She sat down and took stock. "I'm okay. No one's hurt me. I can stick around a little longer."

She turned to the golden door and watched the eclipse and the birth of this fabulous new solar system. The blood moon was still visible on the golden door. Gabrielle recalled. "A lunar eclipse happens when the moon goes into the earth's shadow. This takes place only when the sun, earth, and moon directly align on the evening of a full moon." The eclipsing full moon had another blurred object behind it. She couldn't quite make it out, but she had an idea what it could be. Looking at them made her feel vibrant and alive. Feeling a bit dazed, she noticed an object glittering on the golden door. Sparkling lights were directing her to a golden book engraved on its surface. She stretched and grabbed it. Then, the massive golden door opened. The images on the door moved again, taking the shape of two men.

As they materialized right in front of her, Gabrielle saw two large, ancient warriors etched in a painting on the door. White smoke appeared, and it covered the entire area. A brilliant white light shone upon one warrior. He was a towering, blue-eyed blond, dressed in ancient armor, and carried a magnificent, jeweled sword by his side. He walked toward her and announced himself.

"Gabrielle, I am Metatron, and I am one of the highest in the heavenly hierarchy, a master for a great power, and a chancellor for the celestial realms. I am guardian of the Golden Door, and you are here at the Gate to Heaven."

Metatron extended his hand. "Take my hand, Gabrielle. Your destiny awaits you."

She fell to her knees and shook. She was frantic, scared, and distraught. "What am I to do?" she said aloud.

She turned her head to see another bright light shining down, and then a figure emerged from it and came toward her. A woman with beautiful golden hair, piercing brown eyes, and dressed in a long white robe floated toward her.

"I am Anaelle, Gabrielle. The grace of our kingdom has sent me to breathe air into your body. I am the protector and ruler of Venus."

These angelic messengers entranced Gabrielle. They both reached out to her; she rose, and they took her through the Golden Door. A warmth swept through her body and a sense of calmness fell upon her. Metatron released a flash of light and took a seed from Gabrielle. He planted it in the new eclipsed sun. They all walked through the Golden Door that led to the new planet. Gabrielle's destiny was in place, and the angelic messengers set her mind to fulfill the prophecy of a divine inspiration. The great Golden Door closed.

Gabrielle's journey began.

Chapter Five
An Ancient Civilization

Michael was recording geothermal energy activity in the Bakoni Ruins, and the readings were shooting off the scales. There appeared to be no heat and no extra warmth around him, which was confusing. It was so extraordinary that it left him scratching his head. He checked his phone to see if Gabrielle had returned any of his messages. "I hope she's okay. I don't know what we were thinking. We should have gone together to each site."

He gazed up at the sky. It appeared to be on fire as a tremendous number of solar flares were bursting over the horizon. The light show was incredible, but he was also experiencing guilt. As he organized his equipment, he talked to himself.

"We both desire the sciences of outer space. I know she is a tough girl, and she's also beautiful. That kiss sure got my attention. She can manage this." But he wasn't so sure.

Michael could not get Gabrielle out of his mind, and he realized his feelings for her ran deep. He wanted her close and safe and knew he wanted more, but this was not the time or the place.

He paused and shook his head. His ears started ringing, and he muttered as he moved the equipment, "I should have asked her out on a date when we were at the airport. We have a lot in common: she cooks and bakes, and I like to eat. But Gabrielle is all about her career. She pays attention to Ben and what he would want her to do for the observatory. I know she is doing the right thing."

Michael adjusted his equipment and continued to think hard about this situation, and wondered what to do. The look on his face was blank. He gazed out into the horizons and planned.

"This situation has become bizarre. What am I doing down here, while Gabrielle is up there, in Egypt, all by herself?"

He realized he was talking aloud, and it depressed him.

"Well, I guess I should stop thinking like this and start understanding that this is all happening for a reason. We both have the expertise in this field; we can contribute a lot."

As the time drew closer to the total lunar eclipse, a vivid image came into view, so he walked toward it. The sky was flashing with streams of astral fire; he looked up to see a blood moon. The dust on the terrain swirled in perfect circles, and his hands trembled. He was witnessing a beam of light right on top of the Ruin it drew him to. Incredible lightning bolts were flying everywhere. The ground shook and rumbled. It felt like an earthquake.

"Okay, what is going on here?"

A quick flash appeared. Michael looked skyward and saw a ray of bright light streaming toward him. Startled, he made out the figure of a brilliant man in the distance. The next thing the figure was in front of him.

"Hello, Michael. I am Raziel, the watcher and protector of the Bakoni Ruins. I bring you your messengers." Raziel bowed his head and disappeared.

A tall, green-eyed man with long, dark hair approached him. He was wearing a blue robe. He stopped as he announced himself to Michael.

"I am Ariel—the Lion of the heavens and the protector of Earth and all that is to come into the universe. Also known as the keeper of the Sacred Wisdom. I call upon you to guide and protect a gift that will come to you from the heavens. A prophecy awaits you."

Before he could stop himself, Michael fell to his knees. He looked at Ariel with astonishment and wondered who he was.

"You say a prophecy awaits me. Is this my purpose in life?"

Another burst of light flashed in the distance. Michael turned and saw a figure walking through the light. A beautiful female figure with long silver hair and glassy blue eyes appeared. She wore a long white robe, and now she was walking toward him.

"Hello, Michael. My name is Uriel. I am the guardian of Earth and everything that is and is to be in the universe. Also known as the keeper of the sacred fire in the heavens. My light will guide you. The prophecies have directed me to be one watcher of you. I am a messenger of peace and the divine influence over the celestial realms. Before the end of your journey, you will call upon me, because there is much you will need to know."

Michael reacted. "I'm going on a journey. Where are you taking me? And what is it I need to know? And what about Gabrielle? I need to call her."

He moved into Uriel's presence and felt captivated as they both raised their arms and told him to, "Rise."

He looked up to the heavens and thought about his father, Immanuel. *Somebody up there wants me. I hope this message gets back to you.* Then he bowed his head and whispered, "Dad, please don't be mad at me. I don't know what is about to happen or why; I believe you will understand. Dad, I love you."

Michael rose and even though his brain was still battling to accept an ancient civilization in the South African Bakoni Ruins, his heart said otherwise. He felt he was on the cusp of learning the truth about the Anunnaki's existence. They had not yet solved this, and he could be the one. He glanced over and gazed into a shimmering light, and a sense of tranquility settled over him. A portal opened in the Ruin and Ariel and Uriel lit the way through a beam from Lota Orionis. They led him to the gleaming light, and an energy took him in. He felt a pulling sensation, and it enveloped him in warmth. He saw a glimpse of light extracting something from him. Uriel had taken a seed from Michael and planted it in the mysterious blood moon. His mind focused on these messengers from the heavens, and he felt no fear. The gravitational pull began, and the prophecy of a divine inspiration began.

Michael's journey was underway.

Chapter Six
A Blood Moon Gives Birth in the Heavens

Back on Earth, the cosmic activity and the planets' major shifting were putting on an amazing light show. There was a full moon, and the sun was casting solar flares.

Jupiter and Venus were dazzling in the sky as they were closest to Earth. It was a magnificent close encounter with these fascinating bright planets. Together, they looked like the star of Bethlehem, and today also marked this event in history. It was all falling into place as destined, and the scientists were witness to the most sensational event in history.

The total lunar eclipse had lined up with the earth's umbra; it was hiding the sun and creating a moon. This event had given birth to a new blood solar system that comprised an earth-like planet. The impressive sun and moon orbiting around the new planet had eclipsed and showed another blood moon. Pluto was roaming around in the solar system's outer limits. Ben raised his arms in the air in awe as he took in the amazing activity.

"This is just remarkable," he said. "We have a new earth-like planet with a sun and moon eclipsing, and a mystifying new planetary solar system. This is a spectacular time in our history."

Everyone cheered in amazement, as no one had yet figured out how it had happened. It was indeed an incredible event.

Ben tried to contact Gabrielle and Michael to relay the exciting news to them, but they couldn't reach them. Now he was getting worried. Meanwhile, the nine chief scientists were setting up teams in each country to transmit valuable information to all the governments.

Sandra wandered over and handed Ben a piece of paper.

He nodded his head and turned to his computer. Ben opened his networked communication program and stared up at a large screen in front of him. "A World Security Advisory System is now in place, with coded security levels to apply to any threat. Guarded is blue; Low is green; Elevated is yellow; High is orange, and Severe is red."

Linda grabbed a piece of paper from the printer and ran over to Ben. He scanned it. "Okay, everyone, we have an advisory. They have placed the necessary armed forces on high alert."

Ben took a deep breath and squared his shoulders, ready for this part in this cosmic investigation. He looked around the room at the video screens and addressed everyone. "We will setup teams to search for Gabrielle and Michael in Egypt and South Africa. Please forward to us full descriptions of what each country is seeing out there in the universe. I want inclusive narration on all these new planets and their connections to the countries and Earth. The quest for answers is now in motion. So, we need to embrace this planetary cosmogony and put all the pieces together, as this is a gigantic puzzle. Get started, please."

"We have a great visual of the constellations in Orion." Sandra spoke up first on behalf of the team. "Lota Orionis is sending out a beaming light that is shining to us here on Earth. It's faint and misty, but it connects to the new world. It is purple, Ben."

"That is indeed a wondrous color. We relate to the new world," he replied.

Egypt sent through a message: "Ammon Daher checking in. We have Orion connecting with Meissa and an object behind the Great Pyramids of Giza in our reports, Ben."

South Africa: "Andricia Pillay checking in. Hello, Ben, we have a visual. The Orion Nebula is pushing out a stream of light, headed right down to the Bakoni Ruins. Our readings say that it's fixed in place."

Austria: "Adalard Dorn checking in. We have reports from the constellation of Orion. A vibrant signal beams down from Saiph, and it's connecting with the new solar system. It's a duplicate of Mars, and it is a sparkling gold. It's beautiful."

England: "Hello, everyone, Angela Jones checking in. Orion is sending a signal from Bellatrix, and the connection is with Venus's counterpart. We have a radiant, white planet glowing on our screens. What a sight, Ben!"

Canada: "Liam Adams checking in. The Orion constellations are putting on a show, Ben! We have a signal from Rigel, connecting to Mercury's double, which is a flashy silver. It sure is a smart-looking planet."

Turkey: "Adlet Sezer checking in. Orion's Belt is sending a signal from Alnitak. It's connecting to the duplicate of Jupiter; the planet is lighting up our sky with a dazzling pink."

China: "Bing Cheng checking in. We have Orion's Belt sparking up a signal from Alnilam, sending it straight to Saturn's match. It's a gleaming gold with a cosmic silver ring. It's spinning like a top. What a view, Ben."

Australia: "Jacob Jones checking in. Orion is sending a signal from Sigma Orionis to the duplicate of Uranus and is a vivid gray. This is just fascinating, Ben; a lot of excitement going on here."

Mexico: "Juan Beltre checking in. Orion is sending out a signal from Betelgeuse. A streaming bright light is en route to Neptune's double. It's a luminous blue, like the ocean. It's incredible, Ben."

Italy: "Hello, my friends, Marco Abelli checking in. Orion's Belt is sending a signal from Mintaka to Pluto. It shows an intense murky color on its surface, with extraordinary misty clouds floating around it. Ben. This dwarf planet is wowing us here as it's right on our doorstep. Pluto's moons are fabulous, but they are very unstable. In fact, they are wobbling. Pluto has no duplicate, as we can only see one."

Ben considered the reports from all the countries. "I can see we are assembling added information. It connected these new planets to certain countries with a fine, shimmering stream of light from the constellations in Orion. The light appears to be branching out to us like an octopus. This eclipse is signaling the end of time and bringing us a new beginning. What we see out there shows that this is so. They say any rare total lunar or solar eclipse brings bad omens, my friends, with a type of supernatural effect. We are seeing extraordinary and peculiar things floating around in the universe. Let's hope these activities don't foretell a bad beginning. We all need to deal with this surprising situation, so let's keep track of everything that is coming our way."

Ben then advised the countries. "I will send out two teams, one to South Africa and one to Egypt. I am planning to go to Egypt. If any of the countries would like to send representatives, please send them to both areas of interest."

Ben's thoughts were still on Michael and Gabrielle, and he knew that since he had not heard from them since their departure, he would need to contact their families.

Ben turned to his team. "I need to find my colleagues," he said. "When I leave, please contact their families and tell them they are on a field expedition and that we will contact them if we hear anything. This search is now a top priority. When our feet hit the ground, we have to hustle."

Ben hoped the two of them stayed safe, since the source of luminous energy was pointing right to the areas Gabrielle mentioned in her note. He was almost certain they were at the focal point of this irregular activity and had found the primary source.

"I'm almost positive Gabrielle and Michael have both made a discovery in the universe," Ben said.

Project Solar Escape upgraded to a severe alert. Ben received a report that the special elite forces found a high-risk source of energy, and the Texas military base was waiting for his arrival. Ben packed up any equipment he needed for the trip from the observatory and wanted to get on his way as quickly as possible. George, Jimmy, and Sandra would accompany him, whereas the others would stay behind as full command at the Texas observatory.

While packing his data sheets, Ben couldn't seem to get hold of his sons. He called his wife Debbie to ask her to get hold of them after explaining where he needed to go. She said she would try, but then phoned him back within a few minutes.

"I am trying, Ben," Debbie began. "They should have been back from their fishing trip already. This is making me anxious, but I'll keep phoning them."

"Thanks, Debbie. I'm sure it's all fine, it's just the signal. I will keep in touch. Stay safe, honey! Bye." He hung up and slipped his cell into his pocket. He looked at his waiting team and said, "Go home and pack light, then meet me at the Texas military base. Off we go."

***

The Texas military base was the largest such installation in the world. Because of the alert level, specialized forces would accompany Ben and his team. The world's biggest team of scientists and military personnel prepared to depart from around the world. Ben and his team climbed aboard a military C-M5 Super Galaxy. Alongside were the multi-mission aircraft, fighter jets carrying air-to-air missiles, helicopters, reconnaissance aircraft, and much more. In less than ten hours, this team would arrive in Egypt and South Africa. The Egyptian army and South African forces were all prepared and on high alert. All necessary facets of the armies, navies, Marine Corps, air forces, and the Coast Guard were boarding and taking off. The imposing empyrean creation had brought out the mightiest chains of command. All branches would be of major importance for the safety of the planet and on guard against the possibility of warfare with the unknown.

Ben had, over the years, put together a unique set of individuals for just this purpose, and today was the day they needed them. He had several friends in his line of work as astrophysicists. He had selected astronomers who studied interstellar space and dealt with the physical properties of the celestial bodies, matter, and radiation. Biologists who would study the possibilities for any novel forms of life on other planets. Seismologists would be there to detect earthquakes. Chemists would check the atoms and molecules of elements. Physicists would monitor for motion, force, and energy. Geophysicists would look for any changes in the earth's shape. Geologists would examine rocks, minerals, and the earth's landforms to discover if there had been any changes. Audiologists would check the unfamiliar sounds and their properties. Meteorologists would keep track of the atmosphere and the weather. Environmentalists would follow if there had been any changes to the environment. Archaeologists would then work through site excavation and examine the recovery of past life activity. Project Solar Escape also had the most advanced observatory in the world and astrophysicists who also branched out into astronomy and cosmology. Ben had put together a spectacular team.

Dr. Knight's disciplined, analytical methods and expertise were to understand the origins of the earth and the universe, and their fate. Scientists everywhere would follow the substantial changes that had been occurring throughout the universe. Ben now had a considerable job ahead of him.

Chapter Seven
Placed by Mighty Hands

As Gabrielle and Michael traveled through space and time, they came upon the realms of a royal domain. Brought forth by mighty hands, they arrived in a wondrous kingdom. Venus and Jupiter were putting on a spectacular show by dancing on the horizon and distinguishing themselves as the brightest stars throughout the universe.

The two planets, polished by magical colors, had rainbows trailing behind them. When the sun and moon overshadowed each other, they were even bigger and brighter. The moon's celestial body masqueraded as the vibrant sun. As the new solar system revolved around the new planet, the blood moon was beyond its normal intensity. On the horizon, a bright light streamed across the sky. Metatron and Anaelle placed Gabrielle under the Tree of Life on the north side of the new planet. Ariel and Uriel transported Michael from South Africa and placed him under the Tree of Life on the south side of the new planet.

The heavens that mastered the universe and controlled all its mechanisms had created a magnificent source of magnetism around this glorious new planet. Metatron, Anaelle, Uriel, and Ariel bowed their heads to Gabrielle and Michael, who looked up to see their deliverers disappear. The sky was flashing with brilliant, colorful lights. Venus and Jupiter were still glimmering in the sky. It infused Gabrielle and Michael with thoughts of love, hope, and faith, which became strong in both their minds. A radiance fell upon them both. They could hear soft music and the plucking of harp strings in the distance, which made their surroundings serene.

The wind was blowing, and the smell of sweet burning wood lingered in the air. Incense was ever present. The sweet smell of perfumed oils was near, and they could almost taste it. The trees were alive and whispering, giving the two a sense of warmth and a secure magical feeling. As Gabrielle and Michael gazed at the sky above them, a stream of light shone down right in front of each of them. A lone cloud appeared on each of their horizons and floated toward them. The same voice surrounded them both, despite the great distance between them.

"You are the selected ones. I brought you here to this new world to be the Guardians of these divine seeds, which I will place in your hands."

Michael was about to receive a baby boy, and Gabrielle was about to receive a baby girl.

"Michael, this is Sun-Star who will be king."

"Gabrielle, this is Moon-Star who will be queen."

"Take these children and make this your world."

A mystical flare appeared.

Gabrielle and Michael reached out their arms. They were both radiant with joy and happiness. Gabrielle's baby girl, her Moon-Star, wrapped in a soft linen blanket, and Michael's baby boy, his Sun-Star, wrapped in one too. The cloud faded back into the horizon, and they cradled their precious babies in their arms. The sacred star babies opened their eyes to meet their Guardians. They had an intense glow, and it seemed to light up the entire planet. It was breathtaking. Both parents looked upon these cherubs with great love. Gabrielle and Michael now felt a deep sense of calm. Neither of them understood why this felt so right: it just did.

"I will guard this special child," Gabrielle proclaimed. "Thank you. I will honor and obey the laws of this land and raise Moon-Star to be a compassionate queen."

"Thank you for making me the guardian of this most precious child," Michael said. "I will honor and obey the laws of this land and raise Sun-Star to be a fair king."

A shimmer of light flashed by the Tree of Life. The Creator placed a book beside them, and a voice called out, "This is your Book of Destiny. You will know when it is time. Keep it with you for all of eternity; it will guide you through the promised kingdom."

A glowing silhouette of a celestial being with the contours of a man appeared. A distinctive image, it took the full shape of one man, then separated into two as a mirrored image on the northern side and southern side of the planet. Both images were the same, and they walked in unison toward Michael and Gabrielle.

"My name is Raziel," they said in one voice, bowing.

"I am here to help you build upon this paradise. This new world is a gift from the Creator and two royals from the heavens. You will need to find the clue that will be the reason you move from the Fountain of

Enlightenment. It will only appear when you travel to your kingdom, so be sure to watch for it. When you drink from the Fountain of Enlightenment, the divine waters will teach you all you need to know. I will prepare and tend to all your necessities to survive on this planet."

The figures of Raziel bowed to them both. Raziel was a spiritual being in their realm, a man who knew the secrets of humanity. He shaped the planet so that Gabrielle and Michael could live in comfort.

While shooting stars were flashing back and forth, the new planets were vibrant and showed their brilliance.

The celestial kingdom was having a party in the cosmos once the heavens and their messengers placed the Guardians of Sun-Star and Moon-Star. They had fulfilled a prophecy.

Gabrielle and Michael saw what was happening and looked upon it with understanding in their hearts.

Chapter Eight
A Spiritual and Supernatural Discovery

The air force's fighter jets and helicopters refueled and flew across the Mediterranean Sea. The Navy aircraft carriers were already in position in the great waters, and the crews expected these powerful jets. Amid luminous vapors, a mysterious battleship came into existence. It had the name *Lilianne* etched on the starboard side. As it motored across the Mediterranean Sea, the military noted it and there was soon a strong military presence in the great waters.

Meanwhile, the C-M5 Super Galaxy landed in Egypt, and they escorted Ben and his crew to awaiting vehicles that would drive them to the Pyramids of Giza. The Egyptian army had posted signs and placed barriers around the area. They now stood on guard to ensure that the tourists no longer roamed around. The Project Solar Escape teams had arrived on the continent and were setting up their camps in Egypt and in South Africa. They hoped they could find clues as to Gabrielle's and Michael's whereabouts.

Ben looked beyond the great pyramids and noticed a thick fog sitting low over the ground. He wondered whether the fog was covering an item of interest. His team explored the area, checking everywhere, and calling for Gabrielle.

They also recorded subterranean and magnetic readings to rule out any danger from contamination in the area. As much as it seemed crazy, they hoped that this could be a portal to the new world.

Ben stopped what he was doing to contemplate the situation. He made a final decision and called to his team. "These pyramids do not appear to be the source of energy. Our equipment is picking up a signal further ahead. I suggest we move forward."

Bright lights were shining down on them all and as they moved toward a large, low-lying fog, a huge object appeared out of nowhere right in front of them. It was a solid bronze pyramid that had engraved cryptic images. Silver engravings and top-notch artisanship give this structure a mystical appearance. As Ben proceeded toward the pyramid, he felt both admiration and wonder. But he also remained on alert.

The team approached the door that was open. Ben announced, "Proceed with caution. We don't know what lies ahead of us. Let's be sharp."

The military surrounded the team of scientists and walked in the front and next to them in anticipation. They had their rifles in hand, safeties off, and the chambers loaded.

Inside the pyramid's corridor, it was the same scene Gabrielle saw. Flowering vines climbed over the walls along the sides, and lit lanterns led the way. There was a sweet scent of burning wood. Before entering the focal point of the pyramid, Ben and his team waited for clearance. They marveled at the carved, faceless images engraved on the walls.

A unit of skilled soldiers trained in paranormal reconnaissance entered the pyramid and went ahead of them. The soldiers recorded their findings and soon came back to inform their commanding officer on duty of an incredible discovery.

"Sir, we have our report," Lieutenant Johnson said to General Clark. He nodded as he took a small device from the lieutenant and read the report.

"Ben, you and your team of scientists from the Texas observatory are the right people to uncover an answer for a phenomenon that is ahead. You can all proceed. No one is present and there are no signs of danger."

As they moved down the long passageway, they came to a halt and couldn't believe what they were witnessing. They glued their eyes to a towering golden door that was displaying the same blurred images that Gabrielle had seen.

Ben's teams and the military assembled generators outside of the grand pyramid. They setup their equipment and ran cables to lighting, cameras, monitors, computers, and their various exploratory gadgets. They needed to collect data to report any findings to their fellow countries. Ben wanted all countries involved to see the same thing. The teams setup sky cams to involve the adjoining countries involved in Project Solar Escape. The grand pyramid with the golden door was an exciting discovery. As they examined the evidence, Ben remained concerned at what they had found. He worried about Gabrielle. Tucked away in a small opening close to the golden door, he found Gabrielle's luggage, video recorder, and camera, but the camera's storage was blank, and Gabrielle was nowhere in sight.

"This is strange. I am sure she would have taken pictures."

He played back Gabrielle's video recorder for everyone to see and listen to, but there was nothing except static. Then Ben saw a glimmer on the recorder. The golden door shone as it opened. He watched Gabrielle walk into a brilliant light from the other side of the door, which then closed.

Ben was ecstatic. "This spirited door transported Gabrielle out into the universe. It might be to the new planet we discovered; I hope this is so," he said. Although as much as it excited him for her, he knew nothing was certain. "This would be incredible if she went to the new planet, but I sure hope she is safe."

Ben related this information to government officials, confirming that Gabrielle was M.I.S.—missing in space. This was because they had no evidence of her being alive or dead. Just an image on her video recorder showing her walking through an opened door that closed behind her.

South Africa's team then sent Ben an urgent message via video cam. "Andricia here, Ben. A team of soldiers found Michael's workstation and his luggage. But he is nowhere, and his video recorder and camera are blank."

"Thank you, Andricia," Ben replied. "I know where he is. We believe an unknown entity might have transported Gabrielle to the new planet. We got a brief visual of her walking through what we assumed was just a door colored gold. The Golden Door could be a portal. I will explain in a live briefing this evening. Otherwise, all we have from her equipment is static, and the camera is blank. One of my team members will continue looking for more clues as to her whereabouts."

"We quarantined the site when you contacted us, Ben. No one has gone near anything. We set the South African forces up on the perimeter."

"That's great, Andricia. Thank you very much."

Ben handed over all of Gabrielle's equipment to the team members. "Please continue looking through this equipment and try to find more clues."

Ben returned to the Golden Door. "Here we go. Sandra, please make a note of these engravings from right to left."

The Golden Door revealed an unimaginable number of glistening treasures. They had now become full images: chalices, jeweled swords, glowing lanterns, vines, scepters, and sequined spears. Ben stopped and mentioned, "Who is this figure etched here?"

Sandra walked up to the door and looked at the image that was now taking the shape of a woman. "Well, isn't this interesting? She may be a part of a spiritual or a supernatural connection. I am not sure, though. Do you know anything about mystical cards?"

"No, I can't say I do, Sandra. Tell me, please."

"This woman is the Temperance," Sandra explained. "Although I find it rather strange that she has tiny serpents around her head. I do not know the Temperance for that, and there are other mysterious images surrounding her as well. She represents the balance between Earth and water. She should hold two chalices, but she isn't. This seems like an alternate image of her."

Sandra's voice wavered, but when she continued, a brilliant color appeared to sparkle in both of her eyes. "Do you see her dark hair? She is also wearing a mystical embroidered gown, with her head bowed and her eyes closed. At present, she is holding an hourglass that contains the sands of time. She has mixed a blend in this hourglass, and it looks like it comes from a vaporous cloud in the Hourglass Nebula. I am not sure if this is good or bad. It is active, with a source of energy swirling through it." A glowing aura surrounded Sandra, but nobody noticed.

It amazed Ben that Sandra knew so much about the Temperance. In addition, she mentioned the Hourglass Nebula.

"She is a unique character, Sandra. Do you think she could foretell the next event?"

"I'm not sure," Sandra replied. "This is a strange object to be on this incredible door. We may want to hire someone who reads tarot cards. Just a thought."

Ben stared over at Sandra. "Thank you. I will keep that in mind."

Ben turned to his team. "For the time being, people, we need to keep a close eye on this figure. Watch her."

Ben then noticed strange-looking creatures sculpted all over the surface of the Golden Door, and none of them had faces. Engraved serpents, carved modeled images of a man and a woman, and a dark cloud hovered on the top left corner of the door. Then, two enormous men materialized on the door, and when they came into view, they were facing the team. One was on the left side, and another was on the right. Now he could see them more clearly. Their right knees bent, and their heads bowed. He assumed they were the guardians of this Golden Door. They both carried a magnificent, jeweled sword on their port sides and had jeweled breastplates with gold chains dangling. Crafted leather sandals covered their feet, and leather clothing shielded their bodies. On their left arm, they were carrying bronze shields decorated with a silver etching.

As Ben and his team recorded these splendid objects, a flash of light flickered. The two ghostly images that Gabrielle saw earlier were now active on the Golden Door. They were swirling around the new blue Neptune. Ben and his team backed away from the door when the whirling winds appeared, and sparks of light covered the room. Vast clouds formed and darkened the door. Then the images disappeared.

"This is unbelievable," Ben said. "What was that, and where did they go?"

His emotions almost overwhelmed him, but he remained composed. New images settled into place on the door. Everyone felt a pulsating energy or a kind of force from within the pyramid, and it surrounded the Golden Door. Then the brilliant solar system revealed a mystifying sun resting at its center. Orbiting a new sun was a fabulous purple planet and a luminous moon. The scene was startling. Everything appeared to be pulsing with a spiritual and a magical energy.

As the other countries watched this unfold live on video cam, George had news.

"The sun and moon are high for the scale of brightness, Ben," George said. "Pluto and its moons are in the exterior boundaries and seem to be quite shaky. The outer planets' colors are strong; this is indeed a miraculous discovery in the universe and what a wondrous view tucked away in this inexplicable pyramid." Ben turned and faced the video cameras to address everyone.

"These are my live observations, along with my colleagues in this pyramid. Examples of this unusual activity are materializing in front of us. I am so thankful I have you here to watch the universe and examine this extraordinary finding along with us via video cam," Ben said to the people involved with Project Solar Escape.

The constellations in Orion now held center stage with a power of uninterrupted units of light casting upon the universe. These rays lined up with the new pyramid and the Bakoni Ruins.

"This Golden Door appears spirited. It displays an animation of a marvelous world and its own solar system and a mystifying sun and moon. This presence in front of us is of a heavenly and a magical creation. I gather this Golden Door has a great deal of significance. Let's be careful about how we approach and proceed with this magnificent discovery."

Mexico's representative chimed in. "Juan here. We hope everything is okay your way. Orion is sending a signal. Powerful beams of light are coming from Betelgeuse and connecting to the blue Neptune. A dim light is being sent to the north and south side of the new planet."

Australia then added, "Jacob here, we have amazing news. We have a perfect view of the Big Dipper, an asterism in the constellation of Ursa Major and Ursa Minor, and the Little Dipper. The constellations in Orion are charging up; a pulsating signal is coming from Sigma Orionis. There is a faint light beaming down on all our adjoining countries. Direct hits go to the gray Uranus. Streams of light are beaming up toward the new planet everywhere. Something big is about to happen, Ben. The energy levels are through the roof."

As Ben was examining the Golden Door, he saw a change taking place. The Milky Way's disk had enlarged to occupy the new solar system. However, the bulge at the core and halo remained the same.

The Big and Little Dippers now glittered and gleamed on the Golden Door. Neptune was sparkling and Uranus was shimmering. There was much silence throughout the room. It mystified everyone as they viewed the streams of light emanating from the constellations in Orion. Orion was an energetic powerhouse, a force like no other. Orion's constellations continued to send signals from Betelgeuse and Sigma Orionis directing a magnificent flow to the blue Neptune and the gray Uranus. It flooded the spheres with bright lights, then they disappeared.

The teams and countries were trying to figure out what had just happened by reviewing tapes and listening to any sounds made. Ben and his team continued to study the Golden Door.

Sandra handed Ben an earlier data sheet to remind him of upcoming events. His thoughts were around the task at hand, and he was thankful for her reminder. "I know that there will be a total solar eclipse in May, and a lunar eclipse in June—it will be another blood moon. Thank you, Sandra, for keeping me posted on these upcoming events."

The teams and countries were wondering what would transpire during these celestial alignments. None of it made any sense right now, but with this new discovery, they would all prepare for what was about to unfold.

"Temperance on the Golden Door holds the sands of time," Ben relayed to the teams. "This animation shows the new sun and new moon's placement, and they appear to be in motion. The lunar perigee of the moon will be close to the purple planet, and it should appear much larger to this effect. My friends, having a plan is essential. I don't want any injuries or deaths among the teams. Take extra precautions." The scene in front of Ben's eyes continued to amaze him.

The ghostly images reappeared and then disappeared again, and the team wondered how they kept losing sight of them.

"Where did they go again?" Ben said. "Did anyone get those image coordinates?"

The teams responded and kept looking for data, but they were all a bit confused.

"We will go back through the footage and see what we can find," George said.

Ben had to concentrate. All countries were on live screen streaming to research the data. He faced the camera, hit a button, and sent a ping out. All eyes were on Ben.

"Let's be honest, we're all feeling a little overwhelmed. We are all over the place. But there's nothing to worry about. We just need to get organized and setup responsibilities in specific locations. Once we have done this, please observe only one duty unless I ask you to do otherwise. I will set it up for you. I don't want anyone missing something else. Thank you, everyone."

He turned to Sandra and asked her to set up a list of duties and assign a specific team member to each one. Sandra got to work, since all the countries shared the same data.

South Africa notified Ben again. "Andricia here. We have stumbled across these interesting artifacts around one Ruin—a gold tablet with a glowing surface and strange writing. There is a huge sundial casting shadows and pointing toward the east. We've also found seven radiant spheres in one Ruin. Our subterranean readings are rising. We also have readings of a magnetic force on the rise, Ben."

"Thanks, Andricia," Ben replied. "I will inform our officials that we have found a discovery of great interest in South Africa."

Andricia then added, "The spheres are moving closer to each other and changing color."

"Please examine those artifacts around the Ruins," Ben said. "But let's not change any patterns. Send me pictures and transmit a video of the surrounding areas."

Andricia gave Ben a thumbs up. "I will get right on that now, Ben. Over and out."

Chapter Nine
Superior Spiritual Pagans

The messengers from the heavens had put Gabrielle and Michael into their destined place on the north and south side of the new planet. Earlier, Raziel had set down a remarkable house on each side. Gabrielle and Michael were all set with food, clothing, and water.

The two astrophysicists felt strength in the understanding that their purpose was now through their children. The radiance of a high, intense energy shimmered around the children, and Gabrielle and Michael both noted the incredible force. They then drew their attention to their individual Book of Destiny. Gabrielle and Michael both noticed a symbol emerging from it, which took the shape of a deep-seated clamshell. This was to be their first object to find, and they needed to place a shell on the top of their Book of Destiny.

Holding their babies in their arms, they both looked toward their own Fountain of Enlightenment and walked toward it. While bathing their children, both parents searched the area for clamshells but could not find any. The children splashed with joy and moved around in the water. The two new Guardians would come to realize in the days ahead that the water in the fountain was increasing the children's strength, and they were growing.

Gabrielle and Michael returned to their Tree of Life and placed the children in their cradles. They looked skyward and watched hundreds of brilliant lights coming down onto the planet. Astonished by what they were seeing, they worried and wondered what was about to happen.

Raziel appeared, then again became two in a spiritually mirrored image to them both on each side of the planet.

"I bring to you, Gabrielle," he said as he faced her on the northern side of the planet.

"I bring to you, Michael," he said as he faced him on the southern side of the planet.

"The secrets of Heaven's Mysteries, as well as the Grand Knowledge of humanity. I have now placed this in your Book of Destiny. The righteousness you both will seek is Divine Wisdom, which will help you protect this planet. I stand close to the throne, and I am bound by oath to serve and protect."

Ariel also appeared in a spiritual mirrored image on both sides of the planet. The Lion of the heavens, who guards and protects the Spiritual Wisdom, also watched over the celestial creations on Earth and this wonderful new planet. And he was the keeper of the sacred native spirit animals.

"I will produce a unique paradise in this new world," Ariel said to Gabrielle and Michael on their respective sides of the new planet.

He waved his arms and a burst of spiritual energy spread throughout the entire planet. Trees swayed in a whispering flow and they flourished with natural fruit and blossomed with scented flowers.

Large trees were abundant with translucent branches; crystalline leaves were emerging. Massive oceans poured out vigorous waters into the rippling rivers in a continuous flow.

Grasslands, prairies, pastures, and meadows of fresh lavender appeared, while light gusts of wind carried a burst of the aroma. Many birds of many species soared through the blue sky. Rainbow-colored butterflies swirled around Gabrielle and Michael. The forest was lush and alive, running along the edge of the magnificent scenic landscape in a panoramic view.

The new planet reached out with a never-ending extension of wonder, and all was now forming around Gabrielle and Michael. Ariel had established their place on the new planet during magnificent scenery.

A new messenger, Sariel, with his long onyx hair and piercing brown eyes, wore a black robe and was strong in his stance. He also appeared to Gabrielle and Michael, in two forms, as a mirrored image—a celestial messenger in spirit. He raised his arms toward the sky and sent out an intense connection between Betelgeuse and the new blue Neptune.

"The heavens give you a wonderful gift. Look to the forest," Sariel said to Gabrielle.

He broadcast the same message to Michael on the other side.

Sariel was a being who had power over the spirit of death and led heaven's armies.

As a brilliant light illuminated the forest trees, two ghostly cloaked images appeared to be transforming into humans. They walked toward Gabrielle and Michael.

Michael could now see the handsome man that had materialized in the distance. He was wearing a long, dark cloak. His shoulder-length hair was a shiny onyx, and he had a glare that overshadowed his enigmatic, overcast eyes. He approached Michael.

On the other side, a beautiful woman with blonde hair, and radiant, dark-brown eyes, dressed in a superb ivory cloak, approached Gabrielle.

"This is Saffron," Sariel announced to Gabrielle. "She is your spiritual pagan, and she is under oath to serve you and Moon-Star. Ariel has honored Saffron with the masterful, white, sacred native spirit animals. These sacred animals can smell, see, hear, and taste the dangers in your path. On your journey, Saffron and the superior animals will guide and protect you. Saffron will address you as my lady, and the Moon-Star as my queen, when she gains the title."

She bowed her head. "Hello, my lady, hello, my future queen. I am Saffron, a spiritual pagan, a gift to you from the heavens. I bring with me the most powerful and sacred native spirit animals: the white bear, wolf, fox, owl, hawk, and raven."

When Gabrielle fixed her eyes on this mystifying woman, it filled her heart with joy. She detected an offer of strength when she approached her. She stood up and welcomed Saffron with open arms, then she thanked the heavens for sending such an extraordinary woman to escort them on their future journeys.

Michael met Efren, a spiritual pagan who was also bound by oath. He had command of the masterful, black, spirit animals also from Ariel. "Hello, my lord and my future king," he said and bowed his head. "I am at your service to guide and protect you both."

Michael's eyes brightened. He realized he had an exceptional pagan to guide him, and he talked to him. "I look forward to traveling with you and your divine spirit animals."

Gabrielle and Michael welcomed these extraordinary pagans; they were both delighted to see that they were not alone on the new planet. They now had companionship and spiritual guidance in these pagans, and they had also gifted them with their devoted spirit animals.

Ariel appeared and captivated them both with more of his story. It unfolded to them that the heavens had altered their memories of Earth, so they could now focus on the present.

Among the spiritual realms, the west watcher protected the supernatural powers under the influence of the Divine. Uriel glided down and appeared to Michael, and then to Gabrielle. She also came into view as a mirrored image and brought them both good news on the northern and the southern side. Uriel held up her mighty jeweled sword and pointed it skyward, wielding it with a show of power. Both skies on each side of the planet opened and brought in the universe, which beheld a darkness. She turned to face Michael and Gabrielle.

"The heavens are sending you a glorious gift. Look above and you will see."

Gabrielle and Michael set their attention on the darkened universe, where Orion's Belt ignited and triggered the prominent constellation. In the universe, the constellations were lighting up. The new celestial equator was now visible. The Milky Way's halo was casting intense brightness, glowing as it moved beyond the vast universe. Flares were sparking within the solar system, flickering in a show of extreme brightness. Orion signaled Sigma Orionis and the gray Uranus; both sent out a fierce lightning bolt. It turned the Big and Little Dippers upside down and this astonished the watchers. Thousands of glowing orbs poured from the low-lying white clouds and surrounded them. The force of flashing lightning bolts hit the ground, and hundreds of enclosed spheres floated toward them both. There was a sea of floating spheres on the new planet and many of them drifted off into the distance and disappeared. As the clouds and spheres took shape, Michael and Gabrielle both realized that the heavens had sent them several children to occupy this spectacular planet, and several companions and many craftsmen to help them. Companions wearing white robes walked out of the spheres and along a path on both sides of the planet. They held in their arms star babies draped in white linen.

"The children will grow faster both physically and mentally from the waters in the Fountain of Enlightenment. They will learn the most important lessons of humanity," Uriel said.

Gabrielle understood she had many all-female star babies. Michael had all-male star babies. Their companions were adults. All the excitement brought joy to them. Gabrielle's north side and Michael's south side of the new planet were now a scene of joy and harmony. A small town formed on both sides of the new planet. The spiritual messengers had placed Gabrielle and Michael, and their existence on the new planet was now set.

Chapter Ten
Big Guns

Back in Egypt, Ben brought his two sons out of Texas to help him, since he considered them to be his big guns. Considering their costly education, he decided it was time to put their expertise to the test. He announced his decision to the taking part countries and his team.

"The new solar system shows a colossal amount of high infinite energy here in Egypt, South Africa, and in the countries involved with Project Solar Escape. We must investigate day and night. This is the perfect opportunity to bring in my two sons to use their expertise. I want to see what they can contribute," Ben said.

Ben had already spoken to his wife, Debbie, and explained the situation. "I would like to bring Josh and Blake down this way to investigate these abnormal findings; are you okay with that, Debbie?"

"Well, of course, Ben, I am glad you involved our sons in this expedition. Continue and let me know how things are going. I know our boys; they'll do us proud. I got hold of them, and they're both expecting your call. Be safe and let me know what you find, dear, goodbye."

"Thank you, Debbie. I will stay connected, my love. Goodbye."

One phone call and the boys were then on their way to South Africa on a military plane. The team already knew that Josh was a gifted astrophysicist, but now Blake would also bring his talent and his passion for exploring any ancient artifacts from the unknown. Both brothers devoted themselves to the sciences and showed dedication to their work. After all, their dad was their role model.

Ben then explained his sons' areas of expertise to the teams.

"My boys love their work. It comes from their hearts. Blake has a master's degree in archaeology. He has a great deal of knowledge about prehistoric people and their cultures. There is evidence of an ancient civilization in the Bakoni Ruins. This may be a connection to the Anunnaki civilization that once occupied this part of the world. Blake will work on the recovery and examination of any remaining material and evidence. He will study all the objects found in the Ruins. I hope he can offer a favorable conclusion to our questions about the site and what is going on."

Ben continued. "Josh has his masters in astrophysics. He will collaborate with his brother to figure out what these incredible events in the universe are. His specialty is the branch of astronomy that deals with the cosmic matter. Josh is a stargazer. He watches what is occurring in the stars, the galaxies, and interstellar space. He has expert knowledge that deals with the celestial bodies and their properties and the interaction between matter and radiation. What we are concerned with is the chemical and physical natures of these heavenly bodies and what influence these have on the Bakoni Ruins. There appears to be an active root source, an unexplained energy that is connecting with Orion's Belt and its surrounding constellations. I would like to give my sons this opportunity to show us their talents. Let's see what they can do."

Ben and his team continued to monitor the Golden Door that remained peaceful in the pyramid for days. The eleven countries and their teams continued to monitor the data from outer space.

***

Josh and Blake arrived at a private airport in South Africa.

Military guards escorted Josh and Blake as they exited the plane, and the men saw the South African military presence and a readied military car. The driver did not wear a military uniform. He popped the automatic trunk, and they both noticed a packaged tent on wheels tucked in the corner. Blake and Josh tossed in their luggage and equipment and slipped into the car.

While Josh and Blake were traveling along, taking in the vast landscape, Josh mentioned to Blake, "I went to visit Gabrielle at the observatory before our fishing trip. I didn't mention this because I wanted us to have an enjoyable time. Dad told me to keep my distance from her. The night before, I saw her at the grocery store. She was buying a bunch of interesting items, and said she was going to surprise the staff with breakfast; then she invited me. She said that she had exciting news to tell us, but I didn't have time to find out what that was. I have respected her presence in the observatory for over a year now, but I am having powerful feelings for her. I was going to ask her out, but she left the lunchroom to go to work, and, of course, I was stuffing my face with her fabulous food."

Blake smiled back at him. "She is a smart and friendly woman, Josh. Maybe Dad will understand if you have true feelings for her. Do you?"

"I do, Blake, and the feelings are only getting stronger. She wows me. Her eyes are always radiant with the warmth that comes from her—"

Blake interrupted, "Alright Josh—that's enough, I get the picture."

Josh was now in dreamland about Gabrielle. He took a deep breath, looked out the window, and thought about her. He knew she was part of this expedition, and he hoped to meet up with her so he could express his sentiments to her.

They arrived at the edge of the escarpment at the Bakoni Ruins. To contribute to the discovery of the origin of this extraordinary energy, the brothers awaited their turn to contribute their expertise.

"You have arrived at your destination, and must watch for two female soldiers," the driver said. He reached over the seat and handed Josh his card. "Call me anytime, and by the way, that tent on wheels in the trunk is for you to use."

Josh read the card, all the while wondering why a civilian drove a military car. "Thank you, Tadeas Almasi. We are staying here."

Exiting the car, the men hauled their luggage and the tent out of the trunk. When Blake looked over, he noticed two decorated soldiers were on approach from the South African Armed Forces. The soldiers both stopped. Brigadier General Dineo Davids and Major General Azille Jansen knew of the two men's assignments.

Jansen approached them. "May we see your credentials, please?"

Blake reached into his satchel and handed them their passports. Jansen examined them and passed them back and then attached their name tags to their shirts.

Davids handed Blake a special device.

"This will transmit information to the South African and Egyptian observatories and to your father."

"Thank you," Blake and Josh said.

"Good luck, gentlemen." The two women smiled and left the site.

Josh and Blake walked down a narrow path, with luggage and a tent in hand, in pursuit of the energy source at the Bakoni Ruins.

When they reached the edge of the escarpment, it was time to set up the tent and a workstation. They were eager to get themselves ready to analyze and clarify this anomaly. Since they were both thrilled to be there, their eyes lit up as they took in the vast landscape, covered in thousands of ancient Ruins. Project Solar Escape now had two enthusiastic men who were ready to examine the Bakoni Ruins. The boys reported to the respective teams, knowing that they would mark this irregular occurrence down in the history of humankind.

Blake recorded what he observed, but he figured it would take days for him to document everything. Later, he planned to transfer the data to his father and the two observatories.

"There is a particular Ruin that has seven active spheres, and it has a radiant glow around it. The geothermal reading of the internal heat in this area is unreadable; the needles are bouncing above the scale, even though we can't detect any surface heat. We will keep a close eye on this precise area. We have a visual of an ancient stone monument. It is Adam's Calendar. As I'm observing this object, a shadow is pointing upward with celestial alignments pointing to the south and then to the west."

Blake put his device on pause, and they continued exploring the area. Roaming around the ancient stone structures in the vast landscape, they took in their surroundings and searched for more clues. The number of Ruins were overwhelming, but it again led them back to the same Ruin, which now had a multicolored tinge surrounding it with a forceful drawing of an energy source in their midst. The boys pulled out all their equipment and ran more tests.

Josh scratched his head. "We've got our jobs cut out for us. Look over there, Blake. I see seven Ruins glowing. Do you see them too?"

"Yes, I sure do, Josh."

"The South African teams are working in the wrong areas," Josh said.

"Don't worry about them," Blake replied. "They have seen something, too."

"Alright, then."

A satellite controlled by the South African army led a connection to their device, and a light flashed. Josh and Blake then received a message through the device from their dad.

"Hello, how is your investigation going, my sons?"

"Hi, Dad." Blake was eager to talk to him. "Josh and I found seven spheres with a steady range of power. These spheres stay enclosed, curved, and they have no sharp angles. The orbs are like objects of fire, with tinges of assorted colors, and they're glowing. They all have a celestial point aimed up toward the universe. We will keep you posted. I will send you a detailed report."

"Great job. Look at the artifacts the South African scientists documented. They're untouched and need investigating. Andricia said they're buried under the sand; I am not sure of the area. Ask the South African team to direct you to them. Good luck." He signed off.

Blake noticed an item of interest and he pointed toward a nearby mound. "Hey, Josh, look over at that sand pile."

Josh approached it with caution. "Let me brush the sand away."

He did so and revealed a golden tablet. "It has strange writing on it."

Blake got a glimpse, and his eyes brightened. They both noticed another object glittering in the sand. Blake moved toward it and brushed the sand away. He glanced over at Josh. "Look at this huge sundial. Isn't this interesting?"

"Yes, let's examine these objects, so we can put in a full report, Blake. We can head over to the tent and check them out."

***

Back in Egypt, Ben's team had set up cameras to cover all angles of the Golden Door. The view hooked up with all the countries involved in Project Solar Escape. The door made strange movements; it appeared to shift to the left and then to the right—even though this was impossible. Two faint impressions appeared and took the shape of a man and a woman. Ben wondered what was materializing and what kind of course it would take. The countries were viewing images of the earth's solar system and the extraordinary solar system around the unknown planet. The view was like a looking glass into outer space. They saw regular scintillating sparks of solar activity. The decorated image of an ancient, armored soldier with a miraculous-sized, jeweled sword took shape on the left side of the Golden Door.

The team watched and saw a sculpted image of a large bronze serpent materializing. It slithered along the door, then it twisted and wound its massive body around the archaic warrior standing on the left.

Ben was worried. "Let's move away from the door," he said to his team.

They all backed away and scattered. Just then, a message came in from Italy.

"Hello, Marco here. Pluto is lighting up the sky and is moving farther from the sun. Its moons are descending and getting brighter. Orion's Belt is emitting a signal from Mintaka; it is sending out two beams of light that are connecting with Pluto. It looks like something, or someone, is going to be sent abroad."

"Oh boy, it looks like we are going to experience a kind of supernatural force." He moved the team even further back.

The Golden Door was charging up; they were aware of what they were seeing, which was an extraordinary force. A thunderous flash of lightning hit the door and a new image appeared in the west corner: a monumental tomb. White clouds surrounded the area as the image became fixed on the Golden Door.

Then, another burst of light emerged and brought an extraordinary force of thunder and hit the door on the west side. The misty cloud revealed an image of a black-cloaked man, standing straight but with his head facing down.

Ben motioned to the team with his arm. "Laser lighting flashes are embedding these two images into the Golden Door. The image of this man is a dark existence, so this might be supernatural. There is active energy flowing all around him, and this entity could be evil. He is sending separate electrifying sparks all over the Golden Door. Now the energy has isolated him on this door, and he is in synch with the energy that flows everywhere. This is unbelievable."

Then, the solid bronze serpent slithered around the door and sprung off, striking out at Ben and his team. The serpent opened its mouth and showed them its miraculous power and its viperous fangs. They all backed away, terrified. Just as the serpent retraced its path and returned to the door, it bit the mighty soldier on the left side, piercing his neck, and holding him captive.

Austria transmitted an urgent message to Ben. "Adalard, checking in. We have activity over here, and it is coming from your way. Orion is dynamic and we can see a signal from Saiph. It's linked right into the golden

Mars, then down to the Golden Door. Someone or something at that door is ruling Mars by force."

The pyramid became unstable and rumbled. Ben spoke with a trembling voice. "What just happened here?"

On the Golden Door, they watched the large, ancient, armored man disappearing. In a beam of light, he and the bronze serpent went into outer space, then straight off to Pluto.

Pluto wobbled and became unstable. Italy sent information over to Ben and Marco checked in, "Ben, no activity has gone to the new planet during this time."

"Thank you, Marco," Ben replied.

Ben was worried because the image of a Temperance on the door showed the sands in the hourglass were running low. The hourglass was turning over to start a fresh phase. The time was flowing to the next eclipse.

These spectacular events were bringing to view more extraordinary changes every day.

Chapter Eleven
Sun-Star and Moon-Star

Those still back on Earth did not know why Gabrielle and Michael were the ones selected to discover a new planet. But they accepted the two scientists' fates and conducted their research, expecting they would soon find out.

In the meantime, Michael and Gabrielle were unaware of the changes taking place on Earth.

Michael stared at Sun-Star and the beautiful children around him. He wondered about his and their future. He noticed a cosmic force erupting around Efren, who was standing near them.

The pagan approached Michael. "My lord, the heavens have granted me privileged information so that I can understand your journey. This will help me notice a great deal. I know now you are royalty in the heavens. Your journey includes me as your adviser and protector. This is your royal domain, your realm. You have a powerful status and authority over this kingdom. Your star baby, our future king, will have the exclusive prerogative to the crown, but by hereditary right. You will both reign over this new planet for life. Your allegiance and devotion will bring you, my lord, the right to be the commander and chief. You will be the ruler for all of eternity, for you are the Guardian of Sun-Star."

"Well, I hope you stick around for eternity, too, Efren," Michael replied. "We here will need your knowledge and wisdom."

Michael knew how important Efren was to him. He was a skilled guide, and he would require Efren's knowledge, both of what he knew now and what the heavens would share with him.

"Thank you," Efren replied. "I look forward to our journey together. And for all of eternity, you will be my brother-in-arms. I will be responsible for your personal development on this new planet, and together we will become a force like no other, my lord."

The new planet was flourishing with beautiful blue translucent oceans and rivers filled with fish and colorful sea life. Meadows, vineyards, and gardens thrived, and wildlife was everywhere. Colorful flowers bloomed; lavender lingered in the air. Abundant fruit trees, snow-peaked mountains, winding trails, and cascading falling waterfalls made the mental picture striking. These spirited elements showed that spring was prominent on both sides of the new planet, which differed from the way it worked on Earth.

Efren built in the area where they were living. The crowds of companions placed upon the planet by the heavens included several craftsmen. The men on Michael's side and women on Gabrielle's side were experts in their fields who worked with stone, brick, pottery, textiles, glass, wood, and produced crafted sandals, boots, and clothing. There were blacksmiths, busy with heavy metals, and goldsmiths who worked with gold, silver, pewter, and crafted suits of armor, swords, shields, spears, daggers, and much more. The messengers had placed various skilled workers on this new planet and had given them all the tools and equipment they needed to work with.

Michael saw the craftsmen did this work in little time. He turned to Efren. "I notice the craftsmen are making a lot of armor, bronze shields, and bronze swords. What is this all about?"

"We do not know what is ahead on our journey, my lord," Efren replied. "I am doing what they command of me, to be at your service and to supply you with what you need. When our journey begins, it will be because of the Fountain of Enlightenment. We will watch for a signal and take note."

Metatron, the luminary of the heavens, appeared to Michael. "Put your hand on the Tree of Life, my lord, when you do not understand. The Tree will whisper the answer, and your mind will clear. You will see and hear what you need to know. Your spirit sits on the right side of the Creator. A test of your strength and weakness on this planet will come, and you will learn of your strengths. I will teach you how to master the realm. This is your royal domain."

"You are a great one, Metatron; I look forward to our future together."

Metatron showed Michael the beauty of the new planet that was now his home. While Sun-Star grew up alongside the children, they laughed and played.

"The joys that are to come to you will be the greatest moments of your life," Metatron said, then bowed and left.

Sun-Star grew into an attractive young boy, and he and Michael had a close relationship. Together with the other mentors, Michael taught him to read and write, along with the knowledge he needed to survive on this planet. Their small town was now busy working.

"Well, come on, Sun-Star, let's go pick fruit and vegetables for our dinner this evening," Michael said. "Efren will get us meat to cook. We will feast this evening and have a grand celebration."

Efren took his bow and a quiver full of arrows. He headed out to the forest with his spirit animals to hunt for food.

***

Gabrielle looked at Moon-Star with loving eyes; she glowed with a dazzling shine. Gabrielle realized the child had grown, and that she possessed such beauty. Moon-Star greeted her mother with a loving smile.

"Oh, my little Moon-Star, you bring me so much joy," Gabrielle said. "Every moment we are together, I can feel your warmth and your love, my child. Come here so I can hug and squeeze you."

Moon-Star walked over. "Oh, yes; I need a big hug today." Reaching out, she placed her head on her mother's shoulder and squeezed her. Then Moon-Star asked, "Why are there so many children here with us?"

"Well," Gabrielle said, "they are precious gifts from the heavens. They are special seeds from the Creator sent to serve and protect you."

"That's wonderful. When are we going to the promised kingdom you have been teaching me about?"

"We will know when our Book of our Destiny is ready," Gabrielle said.

In the Fountain of Enlightenment, Sun-Star and Moon-Star aged one year for every day. And when their journey began, their aging would stop— as would that of the other children. They were all now ten years old. The companions had helped a great deal in raising the children so far.

Gabrielle took Moon-Star for a walk, and they saw the rivers flowing toward the east. The meadows flourished with daisies, tall grasses, colorful butterflies, and birds flying and singing. They joined their attendants in one house who were making an assortment of beautiful clothing, and handcrafted sandals and boots for them all.

Moon-Star picked up a glamorous dress and smiled. "This one, Mother, look at the embroidery on it. Is this mine?"

"Yes, I believe so. It suits you," Gabrielle replied. She picked up a pair of sandals and handed them to Moon-Star.

"Look over there, an outfit for you! We can get all dressed up."

Saffron approached and addressed Gabrielle, "My lady, the town is now built, and it is spectacular. We have all that we need. I believe we should celebrate this evening. I will hunt for game."

Moon-Star was now moonlit. "Let's get our hair done, too."

Gabrielle glanced over at Saffron. "Saffron, what a terrific idea. Our future queen here wants to look stylish this evening." They both smiled at her.

"Look at the fields packed with fresh vegetables," Gabrielle said in a burst of excitement. "Oh, we can't forget that delicious fruit. There is plenty for our party."

Moon-Star was wondering if her mother was going to make her drink goat's milk again, and she looked over at her with a concerned expression.

Gabrielle knew what she was thinking. "And yes, drink it."

"How did you know what I was thinking?" she said and slapped her hands to her side.

"I didn't know, but it worked, didn't it?" She laughed.

They wandered off into the orchards with their horse and carriage and gathered up plenty of fruit and headed out to the fields to get fresh vegetables. Sniffing the air, Moon-Star turned and gathered a bunch of fresh lavender. She placed the bouquet under her nose and broke into a big smile. There were daisies on the dinner table.

In ten days, the heavens guided Gabrielle on an incomprehensible passage. The children's progress amazed her and Moon-Star's quick grasp of reading and writing. She looked forward to teaching Moon-Star even more about leadership and responsibility. In such a brief time, the companions had created village essentials for Gabrielle.

Both small towns on the planet were preparing for a big party, and the children and assistants setup lanterns, tables, chairs, and a large fire pit. The wood carvers had made wooden cutlery, plates, and cups. The weavers had made beautiful, embroidered tablecloths and there were glorious instruments to play music for Gabrielle and Michael. On both sides of the planet, there was a celebration.

***

The next day, while they were out collecting ingredients for their dinner, they each stumbled upon a small silver box with no opening.

"Well, this is interesting," Gabrielle said. "We will let Saffron look at this."

***

Michael had found a similar box on the south side and picked it up. "*Hmmm*," he said, "I will have to show this to Efren." He tucked it away in his satchel.

***

Gabrielle went to place the box under the Tree, and when she put her hand on the Tree, she received an electrifying vibration that passed through her body. The Tree of Life whispered to her, and the voice traveled beneath her consciousness. "Take this box to your first destination."

Gabrielle looked at Saffron. "Well, this is enlightening. The Tree of Life just told me what I am to do with this silver box."

***

On his side, Michael touched the Tree of Life and understood he must carry his small box to his first destination.

They both secured them by their sides in a pouch.

***

It was now time for Sun-Star and Moon-Star to head to the Fountain of Enlightenment. Gabrielle and Michael searched throughout their fountain's water for their first clamshell, but today would not be the day to find it.

***

Ten more days passed. Sun-Star and Moon-Star and all the children were now twenty years old. The Fountain of Enlightenment had given them a life in its fullest in twenty days. And at this moment, their aging would stop when they began their journey. They would all grow without the aid of the mystical fountain. Gabrielle and Michael were appreciative and honored by everything given to them.

Sun-Star and Moon-Star and the children learned how to read, write, and do arithmetic as they were growing up. They all learned practical skills and worked in the vast growing fields of wheat and vegetables, as they knew their survival depended on it. Efren and Saffron helped them pick up on important skills for the hunt, while Sun-Star and Moon-Star's readiness for learning their rule came to them through the Fountain of Enlightenment.

Saffron and Efren congratulated Gabrielle and Michael on both sides of the planet at the same time. "In only twenty days, all your children have grown into dutiful and kind adults. The adults will now serve as an army to protect the future king and queen and all who follow. The star children have learned how to seek truth and knowledge, with the help of the Fountain of Enlightenment, as well as their companions and mentors. They act and have an inner strength and integrity that makes them trusted. They will act with honor and behave with complete transparency. You should be proud of their transition," they said.

***

Later that day, Gabrielle sensed a piece was missing in her life. She gazed at the heavens, and a memory surfaced. "Please let me know if Michael is on this planet?" They both wondered what had happened to each other.

She touched the Tree of Life and felt a strong vibration energizing throughout her body.

The Tree whispered, "He is nearby."

Gabrielle pondered why they were not together.

The Tree whispered back to her, "You will see him in time, Gabrielle."

***

Michael had an uneasy feeling. He walked over to his Tree of Life, as he wanted to know about Gabrielle. The Tree whispered, "She is your destiny, Michael."

Michael fell to his knees and glanced up at the heavens with a bewildered look on his face.

"Please keep her safe on this planet. I promise you, Gabrielle, I will find you and love you until the end of time."

Michael faced Efren. "Why haven't I thought of Gabrielle until now? It's been twenty days. It seems like she left my thoughts. How did this happen?"

"It is the will of the heavens and is based upon the need to know. This is so you will both fulfill your destinies, my lord. You will both know what the Creator has in store for you."

"Thank you, Efren. Gabrielle is here and we will be together."

"Gabrielle is waiting for you. Touch the Tree of Life. Whisper to her; you can communicate this way," Efren said.

***

Gabrielle's views transformed back at the observatory. Orion's flickering light had enthralled her through a vast force from the paradises and altered her way of life. She was now amid a life she thought she understood, but deep inside of her was a dark secret tucked away. This celestial contact had set her on a different path. Her fate would still happen in the future and bring about an unusual outcome.

Saffron then imparted the news that she could use the Tree of Life to communicate with Michael. She gazed over at Moon-Star with big bright eyes.

Gabrielle grabbed Moon-Star's hand and touched the Tree of Life. Michael touched his Tree of Life, and a faint light came down from the new Neptune and passed through both trees. Gabrielle and Michael together lit up, and they were both glowing enough to brighten the entire planet. A force of electrifying sparks erupted from their bodies and triggered a sense of happiness. This was one of the most joyous moments in their lives. Saffron and Efren had connected with the new Neptune and each Tree of Life. Michael placed his hand on Sun-Star's shoulder. Gabrielle sensed Michael's presence, and Michael, likewise, sensed her connection.

To speak to Michael, she whispered to her Tree of Life.

"We are secure, but I am not sure when our journey begins; only the heavens know."

Michael's Tree whispered Gabrielle's message to him, and Michael replied. "Gabrielle, think of me holding you tight, and you will always be close to my heart whenever you need me."

The Tree became quiet.

***

Saffron comforted Gabrielle. "My lady, Michael is your destiny; I promise you I will bring you two together."

Gabrielle's heart felt warm. "Oh, Saffron. Oh, Moon-Star. He will hold me tight and keep me close to his heart." She then shed tears of joy. "Thank you, Saffron. This means so much to me. My heart yearns for Michael. My desires are overwhelming. I feel his strength and warmth through the Tree of Life. I am his for eternity."

Gabrielle's radiant glow was moonlit. She looked to the heavens and spoke, "Thank you."

Her mother's glow captivated Moon-Star. "You need to tell me about Michael; I have to know who he is."

"Oh yes," Gabrielle responded. "I will tell you all about Michael. But first, we need to enjoy the celebration the companions have put together for your twentieth birthday and then I can include Michael," she said and took a deep breath.

Gabrielle's helpers served drinks and placed the food on the tables. Saffron sat beside Moon-Star. Everyone sat at the large timber tables. The spirit animals were roaming around the perimeter.

Gabrielle put things in perspective when she sat. Bits and pieces of her past life at the observatory came to mind. She stood up, ready to talk about Michael. "Moon-Star would like to know about Michael," she said and clasped her hands.

Everyone was eager to hear Gabrielle's story.

"Well, let me start. He is twenty-seven years old. We were both born on the same day. Isn't that amazing? The celestial alignments were Jupiter and Mercury, and there was a crescent moon on June 22, 1987. We are both astrophysicists, and we love to branch out into astronomy to deal with the physics of the universe. Monitoring the physical properties of celestial objects is so much fun. However, we both have a love for cosmology as well; that's where we study the universe and its phenomena at the largest scales."

Moon-Star wiped her brow and went, "How fascinating."

Taking a deep breath, Gabrielle continued. "Anyway, he is tall and tanned. He has the most amazing ocean-blue eyes and shiny, sandy blond hair."

She paused and looked over at Moon-Star, who was watching her, and appreciated her encouraging smile. Saffron was looking at Moon-Star and smiled at her.

Gabrielle continued. "He is a soft-spoken man. We worked together with the data and lectures in the observatory; we were almost stuck to each other's sides. I am not sure why we didn't go out on a date, Moon-Star. However, we both have busy lives outside of the observatory. It seems strange, but it's like someone told him not to bother me. Michael loves my cooking. The entire team said I should open a restaurant. My mother and father came from sizable families, so I learned how to cook a variety of dishes for large crowds; it's a cinch," she said and continued to explain her feelings for Michael.

"Michael is a prankster. He likes to hide things, play jokes, and tell jokes. He always makes me laugh, and he lifts my spirits. Come to think of it, he is a very smart man and an amazing scientist. His farseeing ability is like a sixth sense, and I noticed this when we were exploring the universe in the observatory together. Michael loves to stargaze, and I always wondered if he would ever ask me to go stargazing with him. I admire him, and I loved working alongside him.

"He is an only child. At an early age, his mother died. Michael told me her spirit was resting against his heart. I knew that was very emotional for him to tell me about. He also loves his dad. Michael is from a traditional farming family and is an American Texan. I met his father, Immanuel. He came to the observatory to visit. A friendly man. He approached me and said, 'Why isn't my Michael dating you? Look at that gorgeous smile.'

"So, you had no relationship with Michael, or anyone else?" Moon-Star inquired in a soft voice.

"I had no one in my life, but I don't know why. And if he had asked me, I am sure I would have gone out with him. Our busy lives kept us apart until now. I can't wait for you all to meet him. Oh, did I mention Sandra? No, I don't believe I did. Well, let me tell you about her." She wondered how she should phrase it.

"Okay, she likes Michael. She always dresses to make an impact, and the red lipstick she wears glows. She leaves her lip impressions on all the coffee cups, and that just drove me nuts. Her perfume lingered in the observatory for hours. Sandra always looked over at us when we were working. She watched us to see how close Michael was to me. So, I used to step in front of him to block her view. Sandra broke up with her boyfriend and she had her sights on Michael."

She laughed and looked over at Moon-Star.

Moon-Star reached out and grabbed Gabrielle's hand. "Don't worry, Sandra is on Earth, and she is no threat to you. Michael is here for you and only you."

"I know," Gabrielle responded.

Moon-Star absorbed her story and wondered if she was a danger to her mother. "Well, let's hope she doesn't show up here. After all, she is a scientist like you," she said, and frowned.

"Moon-Star, I have never seen you like this. It's okay. I promise I will not talk about her again."

Gabrielle continued, changing the subject back to Michael.

"Michael is my light, my knight in shining armor. He now holds the key to my heart."

"I can't wait to meet Michael. He sounds so dreamy."

As the evening went on, Gabrielle couldn't stop talking about Michael and her new life on a gifted planet. Gabrielle had entranced her audience.

"I can see the love you have for him. It's in your gleaming eyes."

Throughout the evening, a magical presence shone upon Gabrielle. They all saw this and wanted her to enjoy every minute.

***

"She is here," he announced. "I knew they meant her for me; that kiss at the airport nailed it." Michael was ecstatic. His eyes connected with Efren's when he knew it was all coming back to him, and he could not wait to tell everyone about her.

"You look so happy," Sun-Star said to Michael.

"I sure am," Michael replied. "I have you, the brightest light in my life." He draped his arm over his shoulder. "And the woman of my dreams." He patted Sun-Star on the back with enthusiasm. "Let this party begin as soon as you get out into those vineyards, Sun-Star. We need to make containers filled with luscious wine for the festivities. What do you say— you just turned twenty, and I know Gabrielle is on this planet? This is a reason for us to celebrate."

Sun-Star appeared unamused. "I am not stomping those grapes." Then he laughed and added, "Oh, okay. I know it will be a grape fight, just like last time." Then he waved at Efren. "Come on, Efren." Efren laughed and walked alongside them toward the vineyards.

Michael put his hand on Sun-Star's shoulder. "We are going to have a terrific life together, my son."

Efren moved Michael aside. "I can connect you to the Tree of Life through Neptune," Efren mentioned to Michael. "When our Neptune orbiting around our planet shows a shimmering beam of light, then I can connect with it and let you communicate with Gabrielle for a brief time. We must watch for a beam of light on Neptune when we are near the Tree of Life."

Michael smiled as they strolled toward the vineyards.

***

Saffron mentioned the same to Gabrielle, and the good news about Michael excited her.

"So, we will watch the sky, and we will stargaze, Moon-Star, and look for our Neptune to light up. Sound good to you?"

"We sure will," Moon-Star answered.

***

Sun-Star, Efren, and Michael began their festivities.

They sat in their high-backed, wooden chairs at large timber tables, and alongside them were all of Michael's men, attendants, and the spirit animals that guarded the entire area. They filled their chalices to the brim with the glorious wine they had just made. Sun-Star looked over at his father and wanted to know all about Gabrielle.

"Gabrielle must be a fascinating woman."

"You bet she is!"

Sun-Star got everyone's attention. "Listen up. My father is going to tell us about Gabrielle."

Michael took a sip of wine and began.

"Well, Sun-Star, Gabrielle is twenty-seven years old. She is an amazing scientist, and she sure knows her astrophysics. Gabrielle's love for cosmology takes her out into the cosmos, and she told me she never wanted to come back. We were both born on the same day, June 22, 1987—how ironic is that?" he said. "She is tall, and she has these amazing legs. She wears high heels that are sensational. Tanned, she also has long, dark-brown, shiny hair. She always smells so nice and has beautiful hazel eyes. She dresses up; not like me. I go to work wearing a T-shirt, a tie around my neck, shorts, tube socks with runners, oh, and a baseball cap turned backward."

Michael heard the crowd laughing. "I had my days where I dressed! I wore all black," he said, and raised an eyebrow. He looked around at everyone. "Well, not that bad, I hope."

Sun-Star had a big smile on his face. "That must have been funny."

Michael smiled. "Yes, it was. I didn't dress like that all the time. It was on our fun days." He clasped his hands when he thought of her.

"When I first noticed her, Gabrielle was teaching astronomy to a small group of children across the street on her days off." Michael continued. "That is why I never got to know her. Besides, Dr. Ben Knight, our boss at the observatory, warned us all to leave her be. He said she is a great asset to the observatory, and he doesn't want the guys treating her like date material. She is a brilliant scientist and Ben wanted to make certain that all the men at the observatory showed her respect. But she is well-liked and so none of this ever became an issue. It took everything in me not to ask her out. But I met her only brother, Zadkiel. Gabrielle asked me to call him Kiel. We had a blast; I took him out on the town.

"When I got time with her, I discovered she is so approachable and she is a vibrant person—funny, chatty, and interested in so many things. Gabrielle has this ability to see things no one else seems to. Our boss, Ben, kept this a secret, but he told me before he went away. He said these visions only appear to her, that I was to watch her and record any signs if she saw out in the cosmos. But on our last day at the observatory, we both had visions out in the universe. And we are both here now, on opposite sides of this new planet. How strange is that?"

Michael stopped for a moment. "Could you please pass me the carafe of wine, Sun-Star?"

Sun-Star looked down at his grape-stained feet and glared at his father. Then he laughed and handed the carafe to him.

Michael continued, "I know she has a bit of an Indigenous and a French background. She told me that the spirit of her grandmother was in her heart. Gabrielle is from Canada. Her parents were French Canadian, with an Indigenous bloodline from the Maritimes and France. She came to Texas to study astrophysics, and I am sure glad she did. Everyone at the observatory is like an extended family. We both share a love of astrophysics and branching out to cosmology. To us, it seems like a magical thing. We both have it in our hearts, and this brought us together."

Michael took a sip of his wine and thought back to his special memories with Gabrielle. "Did I mention she cooks like no one I know? The variety of food she brought into the observatory was so impressive. She caught my attention all the time. I think she did this on purpose. She knew it drew me near to her." They all laughed, and Michael went on.

"Ah, but I know Josh had his eye on Gabrielle. He is Ben's son, and he is also a part of the team at the observatory. When Gabrielle started working at the observatory, he broke up with his girlfriend. I found that unusual. Then Gabrielle invited him for breakfast the last day we were at the observatory, and he was all about her. I saw him glancing over and winking at her, and she smiled back. It was quite noticeable. I don't know if Gabrielle has any feelings for him. I hope she doesn't. And I didn't enjoy seeing him act this way around her, so I just walked away and tried not to notice. Besides, she never mentioned that she was seeing anyone. I hope she wasn't striking up a relationship with Josh."

"*Aw*, Father, he is no concern of ours now," Sun-Star said. "He is on Earth, and Gabrielle is here with you. My advice is to not let him move into your personal space. You are a terrific father who raised me to be thankful for everything. I will never forget what I have learned from you, and you will be with Gabrielle." Sun-Star winked at him and gave him an easy nod.

Michael sensed a great strength coming from Sun-Star. He knew his son had a special gift of perception and his spirits lifted. "Thank you for your support. It means a lot to me."

Sun-Star's stomach grumbled. "Wow, I can't wait to try Gabrielle's cooking. It sounds delightful."

"You bet it is! We will have a magnificent feast with her. Of course, we will help with the cooking; I am sure she would like that."

Michael took another sip of his wine and continued with his story.

"You know, she kissed me at the airport. She gave me these chills that I have never felt before in my life. And I didn't want her to stop. Standing there holding her in my arms would have been simply fine by me because she made me feel so good."

Sun-Star's eyes were sunlit as he listened to his father's stories. He couldn't wait to meet Gabrielle. "It sounds like you should be together." Efren saw this and smiled.

Michael put his chalice down and told the rest of his story to the crowd as they all enjoyed their wine.

"I wanted to ask her to go stargazing so many times. However, just as I was about to approach her, something or someone always got in the way. Gabrielle is a beautiful woman. I figured, perhaps, she wouldn't go out with a guy like me."

Sun-Star put his hand on his father's shoulder. "Well, you're running around an observatory wearing shorts, a T-shirt, and a tie, and on most days, nothing but black. That's not how you impress a girl, is it?"

Everyone broke out in laughter. "I am just kidding," Sun-Star said. "It sounds like you were a lot of fun to be around."

Michael laughed. "Yes, I guess so. She is here and my heart is hers. I know she is mine; I hold the key to her heart."

Everyone cheered and raised their chalice to Michael. Sun-Star and Efren clinked their chalices together and said, "Cheers."

Michael talked about Gabrielle all night. He captivated and enthralled his audience with significant stories. This was such a joyous moment for both love-struck scientists. They had found each other even though they were on opposite sides of the planet; they were now both fulfilling a prophecy. Moon-Star and Sun-Star couldn't wait to meet them. And as Saffron and Efren were the rulers of the new blue Neptune, they both needed to be under the Tree of Life for Gabrielle and Michael to connect.

Chapter Twelve
A Mighty Jeweled Sword

Meanwhile, back on Earth, Mexico pinged on screen. "Hello, Ben. Orion is building up in brightness and is sending a beam of light to Betelgeuse, then straight to the blue Neptune. The signals have split off to the north and south side of the new planet. The countries are now speculating about what this activity could mean and whether it connects to Gabrielle and Michael," Juan said.

South Africa sounded on screen. "Andricia here, Ben. The Orion Nebula is sending out another signal to the bronze and silver pyramid. The Orion Nebula had also directed a light to the new planet on the north side, but the connection's gone. Has anything unusual happened over there, Ben?"

Canada pinged on screen. "Hello! We have interesting activity to report. Rigel lit up and dispatched a signal straight to the silver Mercury. It's quite apparent that something or someone is going to the northern side of the new planet," Liam said.

"Lots of excitement going on," Ben replied. "And, yes, South Africa, we are seeing strange activity on the Golden Door again today. The big, jeweled sword is now missing, the large soldier is motionless, and we still can't see his face."

Austria then pinged on screen. "We have a Red Alert. Saiph is linking up with the golden Mars, and a beam of light is heading right down to you," Adalard said.

They left the area as a connection on the Golden Door flickered and glowed.

Two images appeared—one of a man and the other of a woman — and they were now taking the shape of humans. Everyone watched, enraptured. The man and woman walked right off the door and moved toward them. The military drew their weapons as the man announced himself to Ben's team.

"There is no need for guns, my friends. My name is Osahar. My name means 'the Creator hears me.' We are messengers from the heavens. By the command of Metatron, he has sent us to Earth, and we are here to guide you."

Turning, he put his hand out, and the woman took it and moved forward.

"This is Mira. We bring you our visions. We will help you understand why the heavens have put this all into place. It is a spiritual journey. You can only receive answers from the Divine if He orders it. I will have instructions and information for you, and your survival will depend on my guidance. I am under oath and will guide and protect you all."

Ben scanned the area and waited to see if anyone else was going to appear.

"Thank you for joining us, Mira and Osahar," Ben said. "It sounds as though you are important to the events that are about to transpire. We look forward to your guidance. This is something we need from you, so we can understand what we take part in here. We have a lot to talk about and we will all cooperate."

Osahar bowed his head. "Thank you, Ben, for your cooperation. I am here for the safety of your planet. I will never give you false information. Everything I learn comes from the Creator."

The countries cheered and thanked Osahar and Mira for coming to Earth.

Ben then tried to explain Earth's concerns. "We do not want any supernatural warfare on this planet. This Golden Door has let us witness unexpected events and brought forth unusual features. Most have so much force that it has become difficult to understand and deal with. We here on Earth have the military defensive strategies, but I don't think we have enough to defeat any extraordinary and unwanted influences from the universe. Also, we would like to know where Gabrielle and Michael are, and whether they are safe."

Ben had experienced this first-hand so could describe what happened with ease. "The Golden Door surprised us earlier with an intimidating bronze serpent. The creature sprung off the door and showed its fangs. It wrapped its enormous body around a towering ancient warrior and then struck the side of the soldier's neck with its powerful jaws. They were both on the left side of this Golden Door. After that, a burst of energy flowed up within the door, and they were both transported straight to Pluto. And now

Pluto is moving out into the universe. It appears unstable as its moons are wobbling, threatening to leave their orbit. Pluto is also carrying dark matter around its surface. We are concerned about this."

He continued. "That huge soldier who stands on the right side of this door lost his jeweled sword earlier. It was large and well-crafted, and it vanished right in front of our eyes. I hope he isn't the guardian of this door since he didn't protect the ancient soldier who was on the left side of him, who went up into Pluto. So, it looks like those soldiers were not protecting each other. I would like to know if they sent anyone to the Bakoni Ruins in the same way you come to us?"

Osahar watched and listened to Ben. "I do not know, so please, you need to calm down. I know this is much to absorb. You all look fine. Ben, if you all want to stay safe, you need to listen to my words." Osahar turned around to speak to all.

"I will only announce this once, so everyone, please pay attention. Do not interfere with the Door's activity. It is a fair warning to all that this Door has no mercy, so keep your distance. Soon enough, you will all know its purpose; I will explain it to you when the Creator permits me to do so."

Mira approached Ben. "The new beginning is approaching, so we must prepare," she said.

"Get Blake and Josh on the phone, please," Ben asked his team. "Let them know what is happening here and find out if anyone has appeared to them."

Sandra spoke to Blake, then put him on speakerphone, and he replied, "Hey, Dad. No, things are still in place in the Bakoni Ruins. Nothing has changed, and no one has appeared to us."

"If Osahar and Mira are visionaries, then they are your eyes in the sky. You know everything is happening for a reason," Josh said.

"Okay, boys, keep me posted on anything you find. I will let you know if there are any changes here."

"No problem, Dad," both sons replied and hung up.

Ben asked his team to set up tents for Osahar and Mira so he could talk to them in private. Mira had an extraordinary glow around her. It was quite apparent that she differed from Osahar. They could not tell by her facial features where she was from, but her tall, slender body sparked with mystifying flares. She had mid-length, reddish hair, misty blue eyes, and was wearing a flowing silver cloak with mysterious embroidered images.

Osahar stood tall: a dark-eyed Egyptian, dressed in the traditional clothing of an ancient priest.

Mira pulled up her sleeves and revealed two mystical figures of sparking flares embedded in both of her wrists. "I will send these items on my wrists to the new planet, through the Golden Door. When the time comes, they will leave a trace of their journey."

Osahar focused on Ben. "We do not know what Gabrielle and Michael's fates are. However, this is a predetermined prophecy. Have faith in what will happen; the Divine Spirit will keep them safe. For now, all I can tell you is that when the solar eclipse takes place, you will see a miracle."

When Ben had learned that Gabrielle and Michael were still alive, and a prophecy had already determined their fate, his face and neck flushed with redness. He wiped the sweat from his brow with a napkin and smiled at Osahar. "So, they are both on the new planet. Thank you for confirming this, Osahar. We have been speculating on this all this time. Now we know for certain, and that makes me feel so much better."

Ben asked Sandra to relay this information to the other teams, as everyone involved needed to know.

Osahar continued. "Deep in the universe, many images will come into play. We are the strength of the Golden Door's gateway, and we go to those who need us. You will see the beauty of what is about to happen. It is the will of the heavens that our guidance will help you in the countless events that are about to occur. So, let's see what the heavens have in store for us. We need to understand the journey Michael and Gabrielle are about to embark on. Open your minds and hearts to them. Let us transport a positive energy to them."

The solar eclipse began on the Golden Door. Mira walked toward Ben. She showed him the figures shadowing on her wrists and said, "It is time to send these two figures to the new planet. This will be a tracking device and we can detect activity on the new planet."

Ben had attracted a great deal of attention from the countries logged in toward Mira and Osahar. "Okay, my colleagues, we are going to witness an extraordinary event." Then he made a jubilant announcement to the Space Agency, who joined in as silhouettes on the video screen.

"Please welcome Mira and Osahar to our team. They will be our lifeline. Mira is about to send a gift to the new planet."

As the teams watched Mira, Ben noticed that the Golden Door's energy was increasing. He understood they both had a force they could use through this miraculous door, and he and his colleagues were not about to go near it.

Mira drew in energy that sparked mystical flares around her body. They all backed away as Mira drew the energy in closer. Control from an unknown force had her use her enigmatic mind metamorphosis. She bowed her head and raised both her arms, pointing them toward the Golden Door. The energy extracted the two figures from her wrists and a funnel of swirling wind exited her body. Ben and his team remained fearful as they watched the Golden Door erupting. Shifting first to the left and then to the right, with a massive force of energy. There was no way to stop the inflow of interstellar gases. The robust gases rippled on the surface of the Golden Door and headed up to an opening within it.

Egypt contacted Ben. "The unknown pyramid is connecting with Meissa in Orion. A signal pushes out of the Milky Way Galaxy. It lights up and separates as it moves through the constellation of Sagittarius. What a sight! The armors are brilliant; it is now making the shape of what looks like an archer," Ammon said.

Ben noted the heavenly display and understood this was the preliminary to an extraordinary event. The fiery stars clustered, then they emerged as dazzling heart-shaped diamond and gold-tipped arrows set in a timber bow. They all waited as the Milky Way Galaxy grew in brightness; it looked like it was ready to explode. Then they monitored the archer as it placed two arrows in the bow and attached were two figures flickering in the constellation of Sagittarius. The archer drew the string back and released them. Meissa thrust out an astral flare and carried the arrows straight to the north and south side of the new planet.

Mira stepped away from the Golden Door and bowed her head. "The two arrows sent are now set into their place."

Ben's sons messaged him and informed him of an unusual storm that had erupted in South Africa. They were now witness to brilliant lights flashing down toward them.

"I've seen nothing like this before," Josh said.

"Take immediate cover," Ben replied.

"No problem, Dad," Blake confirmed, and lost his connection.

Ben called them back and got no answer. "I hope this connection loss is temporary," he said and rubbed his face.

As the sky became brighter and the celestial stars were more apparent, a view of an unusual object appeared. Ben asked the team, "Are you all seeing and recording this peculiar object? It appears on the top of the Golden Door. What is it? Does anyone know?"

The team members examined the object. "It's another blurred image setting itself into place, Ben," Jimmy replied. "But it's not developed enough to tell."

Ben took a breath. "Okay, let's monitor it." He turned to face Osahar.

"I would like to know what the black cloud and the cloaked image on the top left-hand side of this door means. There seems to be a lot of active energy flowing amid this great wonder."

"We do not understand its purpose yet," Osahar replied. "The teams are still deciphering the images and their meanings on the Door."

"It's obvious this dark image is not good, and the white cloud around that monumental tomb has done nothing yet," Ben said. "Mira or Osahar, can you explain why we have such a massive tomb on this door?"

"No, the meaning will only be clear to us later," they both chorused.

Ben shook his head. "We're in for more of these puzzling events."

The room settled down. Ben was tired, and it was time to switch shifts. Team Egypt entered the pyramid and relieved them of their duties. New military enforcements walked in and stood on guard. One soldier walked over to inform Ben. "We setup two tents for the new arrivals," the soldier said. Ben nodded his head, and the soldier walked away.

"Please come this way," Ben said. He directed Osahar and Mira to their tents.

***

Blake and Josh didn't take cover as their dad had asked. They observed every detail of their surroundings. The total solar eclipse was in place above the Bakoni Ruins. It was unusual for the eclipse to be in view of such a length of time.

The Ruins were sparking with intense electrical energy; they were bright. The sundial was spinning like a top, and the golden tablet's writing was almost visible. They looked toward Adam's Calendar to see celestial alignments sending out a vivid stream of light with a reflected image straight toward them.

This light was now set into place in a Ruin right in front of them, and the mirrored image appeared; the two scientists could now see ancient writing.

"Wow. This is crazy. What does it say, Blake?"

Blake inspected it. "The writing is Egyptian. It says: A great pharaoh and queen will appear in the afterlife." They both looked at each other.

"Things are becoming pretty weird around here," Blake added.

"A pharaoh and his queen are coming back from the dead? I imagined nothing like this could even happen," Josh replied. "What do you think?"

"This Ruin may be the portal to the new planet, for us and maybe the pharaoh and queen, Josh. We know Michael and Gabrielle are on that planet. Maybe we're supposed to find them and bring them home?"

"Let's head up to our tent, get supplies, and wait and see if anything happens," Josh said.

"The satellite isn't connecting to our device. We can't seem to use it. I guess we will have to write Dad a note and leave it in the tent," Blake said.

When they arrived at the tent, Blake penned his father with a note that said: *Dear Dad, A great pharaoh and queen are supposed to come back into the afterlife. That is a message we got from Adam's Calendar. If you are reading this message, we're on a mission to find Michael and Gabrielle. And to see if we can find any active portals to and from the new planet. We love you, Blake and Josh.*

They waited in their tent as they watched for any strange activity that might lead them back to the Ruin. They had hoped they would identify a portal to the new planet.

"You know what, Blake?"

"What?"

"I am in love with Gabrielle, and I want to find her."
"I know, Josh. Let's hope the feeling is mutual."

Chapter Thirteen
The Golden Book

The festivities were grand, and the former star babies grown, so no longer needing to bathe in the Fountain of Enlightenment for their spiritual growth. Gabrielle sat under the Tree of Life with Moon-Star and noted her maturity.

Her shiny, long, dark hair and beautiful, soft skin gleamed alongside her blue eyes. She wore tailored clothing and handcrafted leather sandals. Moon-Star was a beauty from the heavens.

Moon-Star met Gabrielle's eyes, which were glittering. "Mother. You are falling in love," she said and tapped her hand. She could see and feel the intensifying energy that was surrounding her.

"Yes. My heart stays warm when I think about him," Gabrielle said.

Moon-Star became dreamy and mentioned, "Oh, I hope I meet a man like Michael someday."

"I am sure you will," Gabrielle replied. "It is your destiny to be queen." Gabrielle leaned closer. "So there has to be a king out there somewhere."

Moon-Star had an emotional moment. "You will never leave me, right?"

"I swear to you, Moon-Star. You are mine for eternity. I will love and protect you until the end of time. Nobody will ever take you away from me. This is my promise to you. The heavens bonded us for life. I am bound by oath, and I will protect you." Gabrielle kissed her on her forehead.

They both wrapped their arms around each other. Gabrielle was gleaming with joy that things seemed to move into place. Then she felt an odd sensation and saw a shiny object underneath the Tree of Life and said, "Oh, look. It's a small golden book. This is the book I found on Earth; it was on the Golden Door."

The book opened, and this fascinated Moon-Star. "Let's see what's in it. This is so exciting."

As Gabrielle read, she noticed the book explained the new moon's lunar and solar eclipses, and it also revealed all the active portals on both planets. It showed the powers that would come from the heavens for safe travel through the secure portals. The book displayed directions for magic and spells, from both the dark and bright side that were not yet known to Gabrielle. Two glimmering scepters appeared as images in the book, and then they popped out at her as physical objects. A message inscribed inside showed that Moon-Star was to protect the scepters. At this, Moon-Star perked up and said, "So, are these scepters mine?"

Gabrielle smiled. "Yes, they are. But you must keep them in a safe place. And because there are two, this means you must share them with someone else."

Moon-Star was ecstatic. "This means the heavens prophesied a king to be in my future!"

Moon-Star's racing heart had her thinking about her king.

Gabrielle was also pleased. She closed the book and tucked it under her arm. "I guess this is for me," she said.

Moon-Star leaned over. "This book is for you and me."

Gabrielle nodded. "I suppose you're right."

The book had many faint images upon it that Gabrielle did not yet understand. She looked to see if there was anything else under the Tree, but found nothing. She was about to tuck the book away in her satchel and realized this golden book was important and that it must not fall into the wrong hands. "I will guard this with my life," she said.

Saffron had been watching from a distance and now joined in. "My lady, you must be careful with this golden book; it will reveal many things when you reach your first destination. Your fate will be determined by this."

"Well, I guess in time, this golden book will reveal its purpose to me. For now, I need to protect it in my satchel," Gabrielle replied.

"Can you please put these scepters in a safe place, too?" Moon-Star asked.

"Yes, these are also significant items," she said, and put them in her satchel.

"Yes, my lady. I am sure we will see eyes that are bright and glossy when our queen meets her king and hands him his scepter."

"This is something I look forward to," Moon-Star said and turned to Saffron. "Now I must put aside my dreamy thoughts about my king. Saffron, let's go help our companions harvest the fields."

Saffron had a knowing grin on her face. "Look to the Fountain of Enlightenment. Our journey to the east should start soon, my lady. Our future queen and I will be back."

Just then, the sky cleared; a rare solar eclipse was now taking place. Gabrielle wondered what was ahead in their journey. She walked over to the Fountain of Enlightenment and gazed into the flowing water.

She noticed a large white clamshell floating on top of a water lily. A powerful scent of incense was in the air. Beautiful butterflies fluttered around in the area, and two ivory doves glided down and perched on the edge of the fountain.

The waters rippled with lily pads and jasmine flowers. Gabrielle reached in and took out a closed clamshell. She placed it on the edge of the fountain where a large crystalline leaf appeared. She knew the fountain had given her the first clamshell, and now they could begin their long journey to the east. This was where their kingdom awaited them.

Gabrielle hollered out to Moon-Star and Saffron. "Look, our destiny awaits us. Come here, you two."

Moon-Star heard her mother's voice and answered, "Mother, I am coming." Saffron joined them.

"Look, I have a tingling sensation in my arm and there is an image forming on my right wrist. What could it be?"

Gabrielle gripped her hand. "I don't know. It's quite faint and difficult to see. I will monitor it. We will soon see what it becomes."

"I will pack up for the journey," Saffron advised Gabrielle.

Saffron alerted the attendants and the grown women. "Our destiny is now being set into place."

"The time has come," Gabrielle announced. "We need to prepare. It will take one day to pack up, then we can move forward."

They all cheered for the future queen and the future queen mother. Gabrielle's followers and all in the small town of heaven's creation perceived this joyous moment and prepared for their journey.

Gabrielle placed the white clamshell alongside the Book of Destiny, knowing it would open in time.

Moon-Star was moonlit; the excitement had spread all over. This was the moment they had been waiting for. They all packed the buggies and carriages and tended to the animals, helping to get ready for their long journey ahead.

Chapter Fourteen
A Shell in the Fountain of Enlightenment

Michael understood Gabrielle stayed safe on the northern side of the planet, and she was his destiny.

Sun-Star was watching him. "I have never seen you this happy before."

"Yes," Michael replied, "I feel happy. Come and walk with me to the Fountain of Enlightenment. I am hoping we can begin our journey soon."

"Okay, let's go," Sun-Star replied, and strolled along with Michael.

A handsome man Sun-Star had grown up to be. He was tall and had a bulky frame, broad shoulders with sandy blond hair and alluring hazel eyes; he was quite charming. They gazed upon the rippling waters to see if they could find a clamshell.

Sun-Star searched, but he found nothing. "Just water snakes slithering around, and frogs jumping from lily pad to lily pad. I can't see a clamshell. Oh, and there is a blurry image on my left wrist. Can you look at it?"

Michael examined his arm. "This is peculiar. That mark was not there when you were a baby. I am not sure; it's a birthmark developing. We will keep a close eye on that."

Michael drew his attention to the flowing waters, and, in a burst of excitement, he said, "I see it—a black clamshell." He reached in and pulled it out. "I found it."

Frogs jumped on a giant lily pad where they sat and let out a ribbit. Michael placed the shell on the lily pad.

Sun-Star's eyes lit up when he saw the shell. "Is this our sign?"

"Yes, the time has come. We're going on our journey. Efren said to look at the Fountain of Enlightenment, as our journey to the east should start soon."

"Let me get Efren," Sun-Star said. "I can't wait to tell him."

"You bet. Get your horse and find him. This is good news," Michael said.

Sun-Star mounted his horse and galloped off to find Efren.

When he found Efren in the fields, he pulled on the reins. "Efren. We found a black clamshell in the fountain. Come, Father wants to see you."

Efren stopped what he was doing and mounted his horse and galloped alongside Sun-Star.

At the Fountain of Enlightenment, Efren approached Michael and was ready to advise him on what to do. "Take the shell and place it in your Book of Destiny. It will open in time."

Michael proceeded to the Tree of Life and placed the black clamshell beside the Book of Destiny.

"My lord," Efren informed Michael, "we must now prepare for our journey. It will take us one day. My briefing comes from the heavens; it connects with my psyche. I understand your journey. Soon, I will know more, but for now, we will travel east where our future king's kingdom awaits him."

"That is great, Efren. We will get ready."

"First, we will assemble all our supplies and load them on our wagons. Then water the horses, tend to the other animals, and get them ready for a long journey. Have them fed and ready to hook up all those buggies and carriages."

Michael, Sun-Star, and Efren went back to the village. He raised his arm in the air and stood on a table and faced their companions. "Everyone listen up. Our journey is now upon us; make sure you pack a bunch of those grapevines and those barrels of delicious wine."

Michael had a smile a mile wide across his face.

Sun-Star looked over at Efren. "*Ummm*, look at my father. He is so excited that our journey is about to begin. And it looks like we will drag along those grapes and barrels of wine."

Efren glanced over at Sun-Star. "Yes, my future king. Our journey is going to be exciting."

"I would like to express my thanks to you, Efren," Sun-Star said. "Your faithfulness and allegiance come from the heavens, so I know you are important to us."

Efren thanked him and then approached Michael. "My lord, you need to be fitted with armor."

"Yes. I am ready to fulfill my duties and responsibilities, Efren," Michael replied.

Michael glanced over at his son. "What about Sun-Star? Do we have armor big enough for those broad shoulders?" he asked, nudged him, and smiled.

"Yes, my lord. Our craftsmen have all our swords, breastplates, and helmets ready. They will fit us out with armor."

The craftsmen walked toward Michael and brought what he needed. They tailored him with handcrafted black armor, with jewels covering his breastplate. Bronze with silver trim on his breastplate had an engraving of a sun on the top left corner. Sun-Star's armor also shone with bronze and silver, with jewels covering his breastplate. A jeweled sword and a defensive bronze shield rested at his side. Michael saw a shining object by the Tree of Life, where a magnificent bronze shield had appeared, also with a sun symbol on the left corner. Next to it stood a flaming sword. Michael admired the mighty sword and his glorious shield, and he heard a faint voice.

"Hear me, Michael. Fear nothing before you. Feel my strength and you will conquer all. There will be many barriers and conflicts ahead. Use all the gifts, take them, and fulfill the prophecy, and the heavens will reward you. Go now in peace." Michael kneeled and responded to the heavens.

"I know the spheres that came down on the planet contained seeds that grew up here, and several went to the east and west. I will not fear what is ahead. My mentors will teach me all the skills that I need, and I will use my strength and courage. I will remain steadfast and fearless."

Michael looked sensational in his new armor. He had pledged his honor and loyalty to the heavens, and he was a warrior.

Sun-Star and Efren kneeled and thanked the Creator. Efren glanced up to see that the heavens were shining down on Michael; an incandescent light was encircling him. Michael was the leader of heaven's army; he looked magnificent. As Michael approached his now-matured family of men, he said, "Please kneel and we will say a prayer to our Creator."

They all bent a knee to the ground and bowed their heads. Michael led them in prayer.

"Let us pray to our Creator's sacred heart. We ask you to guide us with your strength throughout this journey and protect us from sin. We bring forth our allegiance and swear to protect all who live in this divine kingdom. Your strength will bring us to battle and help us defeat all that is evil. We will live our brand-new beginning in peace and harmony, to cherish, love, and have faith in all of humanity in this new kingdom. Amen."

Sariel, Commander of heaven's army, became visible to Michael.

"You are the Guardian of Sun-Star. I will safeguard you both so that no messengers or attendants will stray off their path. Behold my name, Sariel. I will write it on all the shields of your fighting force."

A spark shone and a flickering light engraved Sariel's name on all their bronze shields, which now united them.

"I am at your command, Lord Michael. Raise your shield and call upon me when the time comes. I will serve you and your army." Sariel then vanished.

Michael admired his bronze shield and saw the magnificent emblem of Sariel and a sun. He had placed it upon every single person's shields. Michael, Sun-Star, and Efren continued preparing for their journey. Sun-Star took the reins of two horses and walked over to Michael.

"Let's go for a ride along the riverbank before we leave."

They trotted off all the way through the meadows to the riverbank to water their horses and wait for the shell to open.

Michael chose this occasion to reveal himself to Sun-Star. "I am not your real father, Sun-Star. I am your Guardian."

Sun-Star answered him, "I know. We are both seeds from the heavens. You are a sacred seed. The Creator selected you. Nobody can take your place. You are my heart and soul. You are my real father."

Michael realized how important his life was now with Sun-Star, and how close they had become in only twenty days.

Chapter Fifteen
Inseparable Talismans

The eclipse was now taking place. It was a rare solar eclipse that lasted longer than usual. They wondered why the sky was still bright. It made little sense that the moon and the sun were still passing together across the new planet. In ancient and modern cultures, solar and lunar eclipses might have an advantage for a supernatural cause or a bad omen.

Dazzling stars were on the horizon. Moon-Star walked with her mother and saw that the Book of Destiny was glowing.

On the opposite side of the planet, Sun-Star got a glimpse of an object underneath the Tree of Life and brought it to Michael's attention. Indeed, it was a shimmering object. Under both Michael and Gabrielle's Trees of Life, was a special gift for them. Two circular talismans had odd extensions—handcrafted and made of leather and fine linen woven together to make them inseparable. The images on one side of the talismans were indistinct, while on the other side were symbols of the sun and moon. Gabrielle and Michael pondered if these talismans were an indicator of why they were here. Each picked one up and placed it around their necks. These were their sacred talismans, sent to them by the Creator.

Birds sang as the wind whirled. Then a strong breeze touched them, and they both had to catch their breath. Soon a wonderful feeling of warmth and compassion overcame them, making them aware of a spirit's kindness. Two doves were in flight with twigs in their beaks; they landed and walked toward them both, dropping their twigs on the ground for Gabrielle and Michael. Both realized this was a reminder of where they first started. They picked up the twigs and put them in their satchels. Gabrielle and Michael both knew the twigs belonged in the new kingdom.

Gabrielle and Michael beheld the heavens. "Thank you," they both said.

They would never forget this place. Their blessings from the heavens left them both grateful for their new beginnings with Sun-Star and Moon-Star.

The clouds receded and in spiraled a stream of light, which brightened the land. Raguelle, a celestial being, came into Gabrielle's view. She had silver eyes, a black cloak, and long, dark hair. Raguelle was a prominent leader in the heavens.

She bowed her head to Gabrielle. "My duties are to take vengeance on the luminaries who have transgressed the sacred laws."

Raguelle brought a course of fire, which would annihilate the dark seeds on the planet. The heavens honored her with a distinct power against those who waged war.

"I will help you practice your spiritual disciplines, and then I will teach you the skills you will need on your travels. I am a watcher of you, Gabrielle. When you reach your first destination, you will feel the divine nirvana. I will teach you and Moon-Star the art of warfare."

Gabrielle met a skilled woman who was from the heavens. "Thank you, Raguelle, for your visit. Moon-Star and I look forward to future meetings."

Saffron walked toward Gabrielle and bowed. "My lady, I bring to you your sacred native spirit animals. They are now enlightened and instructed by the Creator to guard and protect my future queen and my lady on your journey."

On the other side, Efren approached Michael and Sun-Star and bowed. "I come with your spirit animals. They are ready to protect you and our future king, my lord."

The spirit animals' eyes sparkled like superb stars. Their fur was smooth and silken. Their stance and vitality spoke of authority. They stood strong and ready, their torsos thick and muscular, their wings long and wide. They were an impressive and mighty force. The spirit animals would be another source of their protection on their journey. Michael and Gabrielle thanked Saffron and Efren for all they had done in twenty days to prepare them for their long journeys. They had both joined in with their companions to prepare the animals, the supplies needed, and much more.

Gabrielle directed her attention to the beautiful spirit animals. "We will cloak their friendship and hold them close to our hearts. We are all family."

***

On the southern side, a brilliant black owl was in flight; its wingspan was huge. Sun-Star extended his left arm, and the splendid creature flew toward him with a powerful, whooshing sound. When it perched on his forearm, Sun-Star was thrilled. "My owl is exquisite," he said to Michael.

"Yes, Sun-Star, what a wondrous gift. This owl is beautiful."

***

Moon-Star raised her right arm, and a white owl with glimmering eyes flew toward her with an effortless force. The owl perched itself on her forearm.

"Look how elegant she is."

Gabrielle responded, "She is magnificent."

The spirit animals walked alongside Gabrielle, each showing its beauty and power. Michael's spirit animals gleamed. A powerful love from their spirit animals fell upon them both. The ravens and hawks flew high above; they looked down on the celestial paradise with their watchful eyes.

Gabrielle and Moon-Star were now being suited with armor—white and jeweled and trimmed with silver and bronze. An engraved moon symbol appeared on the right side of all their breastplates. A glint of light brought down an enormous shadow beyond, and a jeweled sword came into view. Metatron glided toward Gabrielle. "We do not know what forces will come to this heavenly kingdom, Gabrielle. I give you my mighty sword so that it may serve and protect you. When you hold this sword, you will feel an energy within. That is when you will know how to control it."

A sensational amount of high energy was apparent on the horizon. Gazing up into the sky, they all noticed it was brighter than before. This had caught everyone's attention. They all turned and watched to see what was about to transpire. The new sun was sending down a series of solar flares, and as they were hitting the ground, the new planet rumbled. Sariel appeared from a cloud of swirling stardust, and he emerged with an extraordinary glow around him. He walked toward Gabrielle and presented her with a mighty silver shield with his symbol engraved across the top left corner. Gabrielle took the shield. Her eyes brightened as she noticed the top right corner revealed a moon. Sariel turned and raised his arms and sent out an astral flare. They saw a magical flame heading toward all their shields. Gabrielle, Moon-Star, and her female army were now carrying Sariel's sacred symbol and a moon symbol.

"Raise your shield, my lady," Sariel said. "Look to the heavens and call to me when you need me. This shield will bring you the force of a righteous power. In time, you will learn how to use this gift." Sariel finished and bowed.

Gabrielle couldn't believe what was happening. Sariel had placed his symbol on their mighty silver shields, and Gabrielle had received a superior gift from Metatron, as the greatest sword of the spiritual domain. "I am honored to carry your sword, Metatron," she said. "Sariel, your symbol is the highest in the celestial army. Thank you both for these wonderful gifts."

Metatron and Sariel had placed their combined strengths in both the shield and her sword; these gifts would keep her strong. Gabrielle was about to become a fearless warrior for the heavens.

"Let me hear your voice if you appear confused, so we can clear your mind and prepare you for what is ahead," Sariel said.

"I am prepared for my destiny, Sariel," Gabrielle replied. "I can feel the mightiness of this sword and shield, and I thank you."

The messengers drifted away. Gabrielle approached Moon-Star, took her hand, and they went for a walk. Gabrielle knew she would have to tell her about her parentage one day.

"Moon-Star, you know I love you, but I am not your actual mother. I am your Guardian."

Moon-Star gazed into her eyes. "I know. I am a divine creation, delivered to you. We are both seeds of a spiritual creation, but they placed your seed on Earth. The Creator selected you. You are a sacred seed, and you will always be my genuine mother."

Moon-Star smiled and walked alongside Gabrielle; she was in deep thought about her.

***

Michael and Gabrielle suited up with the finest majestic armor. Their royal children had grown to adulthood, and Sun-Star and Moon-Star looked magnificent. They had received their mighty weapons from the spiritual world, and they had learned a great deal from the messengers: their spiritual mentors. Gabrielle and Michael were now ready to travel over this royal and mystical domain. A new kingdom awaited them. And they knew their spiritual mentors would support them throughout their journey. The messengers placed another mindset, as they had been preparing them all along. This was to settle them into an awareness that this planet might not be what they expected.

Chapter Sixteen
A Discovery of Real Love

As the messengers drifted away, it was because they knew Gabrielle and Michael were raring to go.

Saffron sauntered over to Gabrielle and Efren to Michael, and they told them: "You can connect to each other via the Tree of Life for a brief time before we head out on our journey."

Gabrielle gazed at Saffron. Michael stared at the Tree of Life. Then he turned toward Efren, who was now bowing his head. They were both excited, and each ran to their Tree of Life. Both Saffron and Efren beheld the sky, connected with the stunning new blue Neptune, and established an interplanetary signal. Gabrielle and Michael accepted this, and a beaming light from Orion struck them. It radiated at the center of their vision; the stars were shining on them. Next, Gabrielle and Michael saw an object revealing itself in the angelic universe. It spread out the Orion constellation in the cosmos. They both now felt an intimacy and a warm feeling of tenderness. The Trees of Life whispered to them both. Their minds opened to a new dawn as they connected in love.

Their fairy tale began. They were now ready to embrace the real essence of their love.

They experienced a gravitational stimulation from their Trees of Life; the sensational feeling drew them closer to each other. The sensation was spectacular as they both floated around in the air, holding each other in a magical, mystical sphere. Touching Gabrielle's face, Michael slid his fingers through her dark, flowing hair and stared into her glistening eyes. Then their eyes darkened as Efren and Saffron took them into the depths of Orion's cosmic dust. They both sensed a hunger for each other. Their lust and passion were on the rise. Michael drew her close to him and kissed her. Flares of multiple colors erupted and surrounded them. It energized them with excitement, and an awareness of true love and devotion soared upon them.

Michael skimmed his lips alongside her soft face. "I love you, Gabrielle," he whispered.

Gabrielle considered his darkened eyes. "I love you too, Michael," she whispered.

Their love was genuine and was coming from both of their hearts.

When they separated from the Tree, Gabrielle gasped for air. "Oh, Michael, how amazing is that. My whole body feels transcendent."

Michael let go of the Tree and gasped. "Oh, Gabrielle, you took my breath away. We will have to do that again."

Falling to his knees, Michael's hands touched the ground, and his heart was pounding. He glanced at the heavens and knew what he wanted, and it was only Gabrielle. He would go to the end of the universe to keep her love.

Gabrielle leaned up against the Tree of Life. Then she slid down and sat for a moment. She stared out at the now-vacant sky, rubbing her arms, and questioned this confusion she was experiencing. Something was lingering in the back of her mind, but she could not figure it out. She knew her future life with Michael had set. She could feel his strength and his love through her Tree of Life. This warmed her heart, and she desired him.

They both regarded the heavens and said, "Thank you."

In conjunction, Saffron and Efren would produce future events for Gabrielle and Michael. Their connection would be spectacular, transporting them together with a spiritual love through a cosmic connection. Gabrielle and Michael both realized this moment had brought them even closer.

Saffron and Efren walked toward Gabrielle and Michael and announced to them, "Now it is time. Bring your shells to the Fountain of Enlightenment."

"Thank you," Gabrielle and Michael said. "We are ready." They carried their clamshells, gathered their spirit animals, and paced around the Fountain of Enlightenment.

All of them looked up at the heavens, they saw the solar eclipse was still taking place. They set their clamshells on the fountain and awaited Saffron and Efren's instructions.

"Sun-Star and Moon-Star, touch the clamshells and look toward the fountain."

The two-star adults proceeded, and the magical shells opened and displayed a supernatural power coming in from the celestial realms. A glowing black pearl, intended for Sun-Star, and a glossy white pearl for Moon-Star sat in the shells. The heavens had transported these magical items up and onto their wrists. As Gabrielle and Michael watched this take place, they realized this force had embedded these pearls on their wrists, and the faint shapes they had noticed were now becoming clearer, being their birth symbols—a sun and a moon.

"I can't take that off your wrist. It's permanent, Moon-Star. The heavens embed this pearl with your moon symbol."

Sun-Star meandered over to Michael. "Can you see this? The pearl is moving around and there's a small arrow on it pointing toward the east."

"Well, that's a compass swirling on top of your sun and pearl, so that is where we are going then, Sun-Star," Michael replied.

"Mother, my beautiful pearl is pointing toward the east," she said and showed her.

Gabrielle observed the pearl, and a tiny arrow was pointing to the east. "Oh, splendid, Moon-Star, your pearl contains a tiny compass." Then she leaned toward Saffron. "Is this all good, Saffron?"

"Yes, my lady, we are all set," Saffron replied.

Sun-Star and Moon-Star handed the clamshells to their parents, who then walked over to their Trees of Life to place them in their Books of Destiny. At each location, a flicker of light appeared, and a quill penned in the book.

Gabrielle noticed someone walking toward her. She stood up and met a tall male with bright eyes and a wonderful smile standing in front of her.

Gabrielle greeted him. "Hello."

The man greeted Gabrielle, Moon-Star, and Saffron. "My name is Raphael—the ruler of Mercury. I am the shining one who heals all. I will follow you and Michael on your journey. Call me when I am needed, look to the heavens and ask the planet Mercury to connect with me and I will come."

"Thank you, Raphael, for being in our presence," Gabrielle said.

Likewise, Sariel appeared to Michael.

"Your journey is about to begin, Lord Michael. I will lead you to the sacred place where we will all begin our journey."

"As you wish, Sariel," Michael replied.

A supreme burst of celestial energy appeared in the sky and stellar flares hit the ground and broke up into a spiraling galaxy. Next, a presence materialized in a mirrored image of two entities. Gabrielle and Michael got a special visit from an ethereal man named Hamuel.

"I have the power to see the Creator in the sacred realms," he said on both sides of the planet. "As a czar in his order of power, I serve as one of his gatekeepers. Your swords are more powerful than any swords on this planet. The Divine influences your shields, and your gifts from the heavens are now at your service. Read your Book of Destiny. It will enlighten you, then go in peace."

Hamuel curved into the vivid spiraling galaxy and vanished.

Gabrielle and Michael walked over to their Trees of Life and read from their Books of Destiny. Each of their books mentioned they would find their fountains and clamshells along their journey. They also read that there would be a Tree of Life at each destination, and each clamshell would contain a special message to lead them to specific items. Then they discovered the purpose of the pearls embedded on Moon-Star's and Sun-Star's wrists—these would guide them to the next point on their journey.

The books sealed with a spark of light. Gabrielle and Michael now knew that their journey had begun.

Michael raised his head. He took in a deep breath and looked to the heavens.

Gabrielle, likewise, took in a breath and folded her hands over her heart. A tear fell as she gazed into the heavens.

"Are we ready?" Gabrielle asked.

"Yes, my lady. We can be on our way," Saffron replied.

Gabrielle and Michael each turned and faced the enormous crowd that had gathered in their respective locations, and then they raised their swords in the air. Their faces were glowing with a magical energy.

"Our journey begins, my family. Let's move onward," Michael said, and waved his arm to move on.

"Our journey begins, my family," Gabrielle said. She mounted her beautiful mare and turned to her glorious army. "Let's move forward."

***

They traveled along the vast landscape. Following behind them were their magnificent armies, with their horses pulling laden carriages and wagons. Their spirit animals led the way, watching for what was ahead. Their companions moved in formation, guiding the animals. Gabrielle and Michael observed the sky and saw it was radiant. The eclipse was still occurring, and it created a painting in the sky. They realized that this had been taking place for days.

Beyond the eclipse, the stars were flickering. The constellations in Orion were now controlling the universe with an energy that was visible. The universe roared with thunder and lightning. Flashes of bright lights came down and ran across the sky. Gabrielle and Michael just set out; a long journey was ahead of them. But they knew this was their destiny, and they would continue, regardless of what might happen.

"Let's hope our first stop is before nightfall," Michael said.

Saffron and Efren observed the landscape elsewhere and watched the vast horizon with the spirit animals. They knew their first stop would be where they found a Tree of Life and a Fountain of Enlightenment. Gabrielle and Michael both felt a newfound energy; an enigmatic strength was coming down from the universe.

Something profound was about to happen.

Chapter Seventeen
Changes Rock the Heavens

Back at the bronze and silver pyramid, Ben questioned why they had two total solar eclipses—one taking place in the earth's solar system and the other in the ethereal solar system. And even more puzzling was the fact that it had been going on for days.

Earth's sky became bright, and the sun and moon separated.

Ben spoke to his team. "We are seeing a strange celestial object in the visible universe. But the word strange means nothing here. With all that is happening, we need to either change our vocabulary or invent unfamiliar words. This stuff is blowing my mind!"

Sandra piped up, "There are a few more items appearing on the Golden Door, Ben. You need to see this."

"Does that surprise me? No, but please, tell me what they are, Sandra."

"Well first, Ben, I have been watching the Temperance and her sands are running out of time. She is turning the hourglass back over," Sandra pointed out. "The data shows the next eclipse will be a rare total lunar eclipse."

The recent activity in the cosmos and the Temperance amazed Ben. "I wonder how long it is going to take her to reset her sands?"

Ben noticed Sandra seemed fascinated by the Temperance. He turned his attention back to the activities on the Golden Door, where new images were developing.

"Thank you, Sandra. You can continue with your job. I'll take care of these new objects." Ben moved toward the Golden Door.

Ben studied the door and noted an image became clearer. "It looks like a river is running right through a chamber." He stopped and took a sniff. "I can smell burning. Can anyone else?"

"That is the smell of sweet wood burning," George said.

Ben checked out the area but couldn't see any smoke; he shrugged his shoulders and resumed reporting the new findings. Materializing on the Golden Door were new objects, and they were surfacing.

"This area around the door looks like the Nile River," he pointed out. "There is an image of a pharaoh and a queen; I can also see what looks like two pyramids beside them, but none of these images developed." Ben paused, then said, "I can confirm that we now have three pyramids, but this lone pyramid is impressive and set apart from the others. It shows a cosmic radiance."

***

Mira's eyes were glowing as she examined the Golden Door. Osahar saw she was looking toward a darkness that was beyond the door. He knew he must remain silent for the time being. He approached the door and joined Ben.

***

"Yes, this appears to be one of the great pharaohs, Ben, with his queen alongside him. The images are still not clear, and I cannot recognize them. As for the other pyramid on the door, I do not have any details on this one. Soon I will know their existence."

The heavens displayed more images on the door. The team considered if what they were seeing might be the rulers of a kingdom on the new planet.

Ben was worried. "I hope they don't take Michael and Gabrielle as slaves or prisoners. That wouldn't be good. Not at all." He directed his words toward Osahar.

A grand pharaoh and queen were now each holding a glittering scepter, and a cartouche, which was an amulet of protection, hung around each of their necks.

"Those amulets protect the pharaoh and queen from threats," Osahar said.

Bronze and silver chariots ascended, then flails, headrests, and horses arrived. Two Anubis, two ankhs, birds, scarabs, black cats, and sphinxes joined the queen and pharaoh. Then two obelisks took shape and positioned themselves on each side of the two monarchs. Two more amulets emerged on the door, arranged beside the new Saturn. They faded. An energy within the pyramid had directed the team's attention to other areas. And no one noticed neither the amulets' appearance nor their disappearance, except Mira, who was aware as she had contributed to their vanishing.

Ben saw the arrangements were calming down. "Well, it looks like this is settling into place. I guess we will have to wait and see what this means. Please keep me informed," he said to his team. Then asked, "Can someone please contact my boys to see if they are okay?"

A siren called him back to the Golden Door. The team was on high alert as they saw the solar system was changing again and more ethereal energy was surrounding the Golden Door and then lining up in a strange formation. The full moon was visible around the new planet; it glowed, then it began to crescent as the sun glided over its path.

Ben marveled. "Yet another remarkable eclipse; I have never seen so many!"

Mexico chimed in. "Hello, Ben. The new blue Neptune has a permanent link with Betelgeuse with a steady upstream. Extraordinary pulsating movements are sending down streams of light from the constellation in Orion. They are pointing toward the north and south and moving east. We will keep you posted," Juan said.

Italy messaged in. "Hello, Ben. Marco checking in. We have another terrific view of Pluto. It has drifted back into the stratosphere, and it has a dark ring around it. The moons are still unstable and wobbling. Sparks are flying off the dwarf planet. I hope it doesn't explode."

"I hope not either," Ben replied.

China checked in. "Bing, here. Orion's Belt is looking like an octopus. Its tentacles are branching out with beams of lights. It's coming from Alnilam and connecting with the new Saturn. Then it is going down to the Bakoni Ruins. Alnilam is sending a beam of light up to the east side of the new planet."

Austria messaged in. "Saiph is sending a connection down to the Golden Door and straight to Mars, then it is extending to Pluto," Adalard said.

Ben saw the large tomb on the Golden Door was gone. The white cloud had disappeared, and a ray of light was now streaming to Pluto. Ben had a bad feeling about this. Peculiar events had taken place, but this was abnormal for Pluto. In fact, it was impossible. No duplication of the only object that was significant outside in the universe appeared on the door, and Ben wondered why.

"Pluto is playing a key role. I will contact a scientist I know in Africa. He would love to study the variations of the dwarf planet."

Ben continued to study the Golden Door. "It looks like a beam is trying to extract an item from Pluto. There are thick gray clouds forming around it. Steady streams of light are aiming at the west side of the new planet."

The Golden Door shuddered, and a flash of lightning caused it to rumble, followed by a tremendous bang. Pluto became stable and was in the progress of drifting back out into the universe. The constellations in Orion also seemed to have settled down.

"Well, I can't say I know what just happened there," Ben said.

"The dark image up in the left corner is still in place, and we see no changes with the other images," Sandra reported.

"We are going to put this puzzle together soon, because an object just went up to the new planet, and it came from here," Ben declared. "We are going to see things we won't like, so we need to be more prepared to deal with what this magical door is showing us."

Ben glanced over at Osahar and Mira and saw both of their heads bowed in silence. Mira moved away from the door, then Osahar glared at her and watched her walk away. All the countries and their teams were aware of the irregularities that were taking place on the Golden Door. Ben observed his team. They remained fearful of the events unraveling, and so did he. The celestial universe had sent the unknown among them.

Chapter Eighteen
Whirlwind of Trouble

Josh and Blake built up their confidence once more and returned to the glowing Ruin.

There were flare-ups in the area. Blake heard tremors and then saw what looked like volcanic eruptions, followed by unusual activity around them. This was all new to the two of them. In fact, no scientist had ever seen this type of activity. The two brothers were confused and became disoriented. They continued working. They watched and recorded the energy readings, but their findings were not giving them the information they sought.

Josh looked up to see that the sky was clear and had a translucent, glassy look. Next, he saw a blazing inferno moving across the sky and it hovered above them. He could only guess what was about to happen. The wind was swirling and blowing dust and debris about, to where it was becoming unbearable. Then Josh and Blake realized that another eclipse was beginning. The moon intervened with the sun, and then a halo surrounded them in a flawless sphere.

"Hey, Josh, do you see what I see?"

Blake watched in disbelief and whispered, "I do."

Six spheres joined a seventh and made a glowing orb. It lit up and gleamed right in front of them.

The sundial whirled, then became unstable and out of control.

"Look, Josh, the tablet. We can read the Egyptian hieroglyphics. Maybe this will tell us more."

Josh picked up the tablet, a flare erupted, and lit up the hieroglyphics.

"Let me see what it says," Blake said as he scanned the writing. "Mighty hands have selected you. Prepare yourselves; your destinies await."

They both realized the tablet was important, and that it was a part of something big.

Blake drew in a breath and thought for a moment. "We are about to make history, Brother."

Josh looked at Blake and nodded.

Orion's Belt was sending a beam of light from Alnilam, and on toward the new Saturn. It then took on the shape of a full gleaming circle as it streamed down to the Ruin. An astonishing amount of energy appeared within the circle. Josh took the sundial in hand and Blake took the tablet and they stepped into the whirling winds, positioning themselves in the middle of the glowing orb. They gazed upward, braced themselves, and hung on to one another as they detected a brilliant beam of light touching them. They felt its energy as it circled around, confining them.

In this process, they went inside the sphere and prepared for the long journey ahead.

A mist of a magnificent force surrounded them with cosmic energy. They were about to go to the new planet. As Josh and Blake traveled beyond space and time, the heavens opened. Soon they landed on the east side of the new planet and radiant light from the new Saturn greeted them. They looked up and noticed another item had come along with them.

A murky cloud surrounded an image that was moving toward them, and they braced themselves for what or whom they were about to meet. They heard a friendly greeting. It was Cassiel, a man with light brown hair and dark eyes, dressed in a blue robe.

"I am the ruler of Saturn, and protector of the travelers who will come to this new planet. It is my job to communicate with the spiritual world. My knowledge and authority are extensive. You have read the tablet, Blake and Josh. You know your destiny. Those the heavens chose will fulfill a prophecy."

Josh and Blake were confused. "We are the selected ones? To do what?" Blake asked.

"Blake and Josh," Cassiel replied. "I brought here you to build the mightiest and the most magnificent kingdom for the new king and queen. I will give you each an amulet that bears my name. This will help defend you against distant enemies, or anyone who strays within your domain. Please place these around your necks and keep them secure."

As Josh and Blake did as he bid, Cassiel continued to demystify the new role the two brothers found themselves in. "There are now two spheres leading from the Bakoni Ruins, one is an entrance, and the other is an exit to the new planet. These are for time travel to and from Earth. Guards will stand by each of them in spirit until the Creator sets the spheres back in place. Raziel is the watcher and protector of the Bakoni Ruins, and he will appear to you both in time."

Next, Cassiel summoned two giant warriors armed with spears, swords, and glimmering armor. They would protect the portals.

"Your amulets give you the power of entry and exit to the new planet," Cassiel said. "No one can come to this planet without them. I will place these small orbs within your amulets. In this way, I will guard you," he said and continued. "Be cautious. Never take the amulets off your necks. They are for protection. If you remove them, I cannot help you."

"We will keep them safe. We will not remove them," Josh replied.

Cassiel noted the items they had brought through with them.

"You have the sundial; it will lead your way. It's now small enough to carry and is another item to safeguard. You are also responsible for the tablet—it is spiritual and must not get into the wrong hands. This tablet has sacred writings that are meant for the new king and queen, and you must deliver it to them. I will give you all you need to begin your task. You will lead an army of men and women who will come down from the paradises. You will build and protect this kingdom. The heavens will supply you with whatever you need to complete your task. You only need to ask. Josh and Blake, gaze upon the stars. The planet Saturn is your connection. Call upon me any time you need guidance. I will place attendants on the planet. You will have clothing and food and live in comfort."

"Well, what if we want to stay after that, Cassiel?" Blake asked. "What if we like it here?"

"I do not know," Cassiel replied. "You are here at the will of the heavens. Different mentors will visit you, offering help. The messengers are all faithful to the Divine and have sworn an oath to serve you."

"So, Cassiel," Josh asked. "Where are Gabrielle and Michael on this planet? Are we going to see them?"

"Yes, you will see them," Cassiel replied. "They guide the future queen and king to the new kingdom you will build, but this will not be for some time. They have a journey set out before them. Gabrielle and Michael both have a destiny to fulfill on separate parts of this planet. This new planet is the promised kingdom and must undergo cleansing before the new queen and king can live there."

Blake and Josh thanked Cassiel for his guidance and the extraordinary journey that was now set out for them. Cassiel had set the prophecy in place for them both and faded out.

"Well, at least now we know what Gabrielle and Michael's purpose is, and ours as well," Josh said, and tilted his head toward Blake.

"Come on, Josh," Blake said. "Sit down and think about this. Our duties and responsibilities are something we need to discuss. If only Dad were here. I wish we could at least let him know where we are. Now this new planet worries me; how are we supposed to do this? And are we going to see our family again?"

"I am here for Gabrielle," Josh said. "She and Michael are on different parts of this planet. So, this must mean I have to find her. Cassiel said we will have guidance, so calm down. I am sure we will see Mom and Dad in time."

"You settle down. Keep focused on what we are supposed to do. We need to be prepared for whatever we encounter. I'm only figuring out what our task is. But I am sure it has nothing to do with your love life, so stop thinking about Gabrielle."

"I will not say another word," Josh replied. "I will maintain total focus on the task at hand."

Blake sensed Josh had thrown in a little sarcasm, and he shook his head. "You better, because we do not know what we're going to face on this new planet."

***

The countries involved with Project Solar Escape had witnessed miraculous events, and they were trying to study everything that had taken place.

"We're just getting started," Ben announced. "This isn't over yet, by any means."

China's latest message to the observatory came through. "Hello, Ben. Alnilam and Saturn's connection to the new planet came from the east side," Bing said.

From South Africa, Andricia Pillay informed Ben: "Our military performed their passes over the landscape and said your sons are missing. The artifacts that were around the Ruins are also gone. They left a note for you in their tent, Ben. The satellites are working now, so we are sending a scanned copy over to you."

"First Michael went missing in the Ruins, now my sons. Andricia, I hope they are in expert hands; I will never hear the end of this if Debbie gets wind of it," Ben replied. "Of course, I appreciate all you have been doing at your end. I look forward to their message."

George spoke up and reassured Ben, "If all the relics that were around the Ruins are gone, then the sundial and tablet will bring them back from wherever they went to—the new planet."

Ben was now wondering why he had even involved his two sons. It was like another force had made him do it.

"Why do they want my boys?" he wondered aloud.

Andricia then updated Ben further. "There are new Ruins glowing on the horizon; the brightness is overwhelming, but it seems to settle down now."

"Oh boy, now I have to explain this all to Debbie!"

Bing checked in from China. "Good news, Ben. We can follow Josh and Blake. They are both connected with the new Saturn. And they're wearing a piece that's sending out a signal, so we can track them."

Ben smiled. "Thank you, Bing. I can see this on the Golden Door."

Ben was relieved. Orion's Belt had an unusual connection that had given them a visual of where Michael, Gabrielle, Josh, and Blake were. Dark clouds surrounded areas on the new planet and on the Golden Door.

Osahar approached Ben. "There will be times when I can touch the Golden Door. At those times, I will be full of magical and spiritual energy."

Osahar raised an arm and pointed to the door to enlighten everyone. "I can enlarge our view of the area of the new planet we are interested in. The Golden Door will show a lifelike 3-D image. You will glimpse it, then it will disappear."

Osahar bowed his head. Mira remained silent and walked away.

"This is fantastic, Osahar. Thanks to you and Mira for being here with us. We are eager to learn more about this Golden Door and the new planet. It is showing us the connections in Orion's constellation are crucial; it impacts the universe. This magical Golden Door and the Bakoni Ruins are our lifelines, and the heart and soul of the universe."

Chapter Nineteen
A Disturbing Presence

Michael was riding along the mountainside with Sun-Star, Efren, the spirit animals, their companions, and his grand army. Scenic landscapes and long winding trails created a panoramic view that made their journey enjoyable. Sun-Star navigated by watching his wrist as the black pearl swirled toward the eastern part of the new planet.

Soon they saw a volcano and, as they drew closer, they noticed flares erupting from its inner core. Michael hoped they could get past it before hot, flaming lava coursed down the mountainside. He wanted to reach their first destination and before nightfall. Efren and the spirit animals went ahead and soon returned with good news.

"My lord, I have found a safe passage past the volcano," Efren said.

"That's great news. I hope it leads us to our first destination," Michael replied.

Michael turned and raised an arm to his followers. "Okay. My family, you can move forward."

Michael saw a representation showing two images. It was right in front of him: two large pillars. On the left side, a brilliant sun lay on top and the one on the right side displayed a radiant moon on the top. He realized Gabrielle must be with a double to Sun-Star, who might be Moon-Star.

He twisted and faced Sun-Star and pointed to the moon. "Look over there, see what's perched up on that right hand of that pillar? It's a symbol of a moon, Sun-Star. This is a sign that you have a Moon-Star in your destiny."

Sun-Star looked confused. "I don't understand. What does that moon symbol have to do with me? And how do you know this Moon-Star is my destiny?"

"Ah, Sun-Star, you will see."

Then Michael glanced over at Efren with a questioning gaze. Efren understood Michael's quandary. He rode to Sun-Star's side and explained.

"She is a Moon-Star and is born from the heavens. They say, my future king, that her beauty is unbelievable. I believe she has long, dark hair and eyes that glisten like the blue ocean under a brilliant sun. This woman is perfect for you. She is your destiny and will be your queen."

Sun-Star peeked over at Michael.

"Well, that was a surprise," Sun-Star said and crossed his arms.

Now he wanted Michael's reaction. The information Efren had brought forth brightened him.

"This is incredible," Sun-Star said and waved at him.

Michael still didn't reply to him.

"A beauty from the heavens," Sun-Star said as he spoke a little louder. "I can't wait to meet her." He stopped his mount and turned it in front of Michael. "Sometimes I wonder if you are even listening to me."

Michael's thoughts were of Gabrielle. He soon snapped out of it and laughed. "Calm down. I am happy for you."

"I guess we have a lot to look forward to," Sun-Star said.

Michael saw Efren had introduced a new chapter to his son, and he smiled. He gave Sun-Star a tap on his shoulder. "We do. Let's continue through those pillars," Michael said, and pointed the way.

A large waterfall became visible alongside the pillars. The water was rippling and flowing along mossy rocks, and rainbows were in the mist. Efren had a secret energy that regulated his magic. His magic was on a supernatural and a spiritual level. His spectral eyes and power took him beyond the solar system to engage with the new Neptune. He had planned the waters that flowed on the new planet. He was a powerhouse and would display his forces on this new planet. When he raised his arms, the atmosphere was brighter. The energy from his body pushed toward the waterfall. He made the sign of a bronze pentagram, and it burned through a magical fire in the steady flow of water. He opened the waters, causing them to recede on the right and left, creating a path along the riverbed. The burning pentagram remained lit over the waters along each bank, ensuring a constant flow. With his spiritual fire, it would ward any source of evil off, but not for long.

"Impressive, Efren," Michael said. "Your magic is going to be of tremendous value to us. What do you think, Sun-Star?"

"Oh, you bet I am impressed," Sun-Star said.

Efren then noticed a complete change in Sun-Star. He was now eager to reach his destiny.

Michael saw Efren was wearing a shiny bronze pentacle around his neck. "I didn't notice that around your neck before; where did it come from?" he said.

Sun-Star had seen a path ahead and sat up in his saddle. "Look, there's a pathway beside those large trees."

The forest had a sense of motion; vines crawled up the side of their trunks, making them seem alive. As they rode past the river, they met dark clouds drifting beyond. There was a large bronze gate in the distance, which glistened with colorful images.

Michael felt a bit confused. "There seems to be a kind of energy flowing through this gate." He stared at strange images whose outlines were becoming clearer through a mysterious energy flowing through the gate. They dismounted their horses and approached the mysterious bronze gate.

"Do not touch this gate for now," Efren said. "I will let you know when it is safe."

They saw strange figures at the gate, so they moved closer to examine them. They could make out curious-looking, blurred images that floated around the clouds and serpents slithering over them. Enormous bird-like bats appeared, then they noticed a chalice pouring water into a river that flowed toward oceans. An enchanting mermaid with glistening eyes stared down at them. Wizard wands sparked flares and there were knives, black swords, ships with enormous sails, and shadowy shields bearing unknown emblems in another area. Pentacles rose out of the ground and a man with six cups floating around him. A faint image of a key appeared and started rising off the gate.

Michael's attention stayed on the strange images. He asked Efren and Sun-Star, "Can you figure out who this might be? It looks like a man, but just the round part of his face is showing. I can't see his eyes as they're closed. He is the color of brilliant bronze. In fact, he's gold. He is wearing an interesting amulet around his neck and holds a scepter in his hand. This may be a deity of great power; a pharaoh."

Efren inspected the image on the gate. "I believe this unknown image may come to us in the future, my lord. I will keep this in mind. If he should fall upon our path, we will be cautious."

The gate held a great deal of interest for Michael. It was a supernatural barrier, and he wondered if he wanted to open it.

He had to decide. As he looked upward, he noticed the sky was getting darker and the solar storm was getting worse. They were all moving even closer to the door when something caught their attention. The black pearl on Sun-Star's arm moved and pointed to a key, which Sun-Star assumed opened the gate. He showed his father, and Michael addressed Efren, who nodded his head.

Sun-Star reached for the key and handed it to Michael.

"This key is huge. However, I don't see a keyhole?"

Michael had his eyes locked on the gate when a huge keyhole came into sight. The bronze gate took a different shape. It was alive.

A mermaid began beckoning to Sun-Star. He became curious and moved closer to her. She extended her hand toward him, and he reached out to her.

Efren reacted. "Back away. This door is not safe." Sun-Star moved back, still staring into the mermaid's eyes.

Efren recognized Sun-Star might get tricked. He watched him, then walked in front of him and blocked his view. "Please, look away from her. Do not let her captivate you with her stare. Do you understand?"

Sun-Star bowed his head. "Yes, Efren, I see I have already fallen into a trap."

Efren put an arm around Sun-Star's shoulder. "You are going to be fine. Just remember to look away and let us know if you sense or feel as if your mind is being taken over."

"On our journey, I will never leave my father's or your side," Sun-Star said.

Michael also noticed that Sun-Star became entranced. "We will protect you. This is not an isolated incident. There is more to come. So you need to be aware and stay focused. Look at me when you consider something you do not understand. Believe me, I understand your bewildered look," he said, and raised an eyebrow. "Save yourself for Moon-Star and never mind about that mermaid."

Efren laughed. "He will be okay, my lord. She is quite entrancing, if I say so myself. I hope we don't meet up with her again."

A man dressed in a Fool's outfit jumped off the gate and said, "Hello."

Efren and the army circled Lord Michael and their future king. The sound of raw steel pulled from scabbards echoed around them and they raised their shields. The odd little man had startled them.

Michael gasped. "Who are you?"

The strange man bowed. "I am Dante; your Fool," he replied.

Dante had red hair and gray eyes. He was wearing a spectacular Fool's outfit.

"I am being commanded by the heavens to bring you to your new beginning, my lord. Here are your four elements for this fabulous new planet."

Michael leaned over to Efren. "Is this true, Efren? Is this encounter with this strange-looking man safe?"

"Let me look at him, my lord."

Efren approached Dante and then glared into his shadowy gray eyes, and he grasped onto a vision. He smiled and nodded, as he knew who had sent this man to Michael. "Yes, my lord. This is a good man—foolish, but good. He is on our side."

Flares encompassed Dante's body.

He approached Sun-Star. "I bring to you, my future king, the intensity of your fire." Then he bowed before Sun-Star and handed him an actual fireball. The fireball rooted on Sun-Star's wrist, and it surrounded his symbols, sparking radiant flares.

Turning his attention to Michael, he said, "For you, my lord, I bring a spinning whirlwind so your mighty sword will swing in all directions." Michael felt a surge of energy entering his body. Then Dante bowed before Lord Michael.

He stood up and, looking into Efren's dark eyes, Dante bowed once more. "I bring you a drop of water, Efren. This represents the magnificent waters on this new planet, and it will add to your powers."

Dante turned back to Michael. "As for the pentacles, I will mount them on all your shields, alongside Sariel's mark, to represent the land you walk upon. It is an honor to you that Sariel is on all the shields. He is the spirit of death, leader of heaven's army, and at the command of the heavens. His protective powers are bound by oath to you. Sariel is sacred and a mighty warrior." Dante took a breath and continued.

"Your fifth element is the magic that comes when you get enlightened by the Creator. It will extend to the other symbols of power on your shields. Last, I give you these six chalices. They need to be brought to the new palace."

Dante fixed his eyes on Michael. "My lord. I heard you are now the leader of heaven's army, and Sariel is an equal and he is by your side. You are one of the most important warriors on this planet and soon to be bound by an oath. The prophecy reads that Sun-Star is the new king of this new planet, and you are his Guardian."

"Yes, I already know that. What else should we know about you, Dante?" Michael asked the redheaded man.

"I am to follow you on your journey. I am your Fool, the one who brings you your new beginning, my lord."

"Efren, please tell me what you think?"

"This is your path and this man, Dante, is to follow us on our journey."

"Okay, army, saddle him up," Michael said as he waved his arm.

Everyone was staring at Michael. "Are we ready to open this gate, my lord?" Efren said.

"Yes, Father, enough already," Sun-Star said. "We have to continue."

Just as Michael was about to open the gate, Metatron appeared before them. The images on the gate stopped moving as if frozen in time, and the large bronze gate became lifeless.

"This gate leads to the tombs of the uncharted," Metatron said.

"When it opens, the spirits will rise and flee. You have the power, my lord. Move forward without fear of the unknown. Sariel will be by your side to guide and help you lead your army. Raise your sword, Lord Michael, so the heavens know you are ready."

Michael raised his sword. Flames and lightning rose and shot toward the universe. Michael looked valiant; his sword was glowing. He turned to Metatron and bowed his head. "Metatron, your presence is a great inspiration to me. I feel your strength. Thank you for this visit."

Metatron bowed to Michael and vanished.

"We will not fear what is ahead," Michael announced to his army. "We are the Guardians of this new planet, and I will soon be bound by an oath to protect my son, our future king. You are all my brothers in arms. I will protect you as best as the heavens will allow me. I will fight until death, my loyal warriors."

Michael's army cheered loud enough it reached the opposite side of the planet. The army wore dark armor, and their mounts were glorious black stallions. Bronze swords were by their port sides, and they carried striking bronze shields. They raised their swords and acknowledged Michael's words of wisdom. "Hail to our mighty future king, hail to the future king's father, Lord Michael."

Michael felt a chill run up and down his spine as his army and followers cheered. He understood he had greatness in his presence. Again, he turned to Efren. "These men were once my children, sent to me from the heavens. Our companions helped us raise them, Efren. The children here on this new planet are the celestial army I now rule."

"Yes, my lord," Efren replied.

Michael pointed his sword at his men. "I am your leader," he declared. "Any man who follows me and perishes in battle will go back to the heavens. Hear me, our Creator, that I may give all followers of both myself and Gabrielle, and any sacred seeds you have planted an ultimate resting place."

Michael saw a flash of light stream across the horizon; a white cloud circled the entire planet. Then the cloud receded to the north and stayed in the south. The Creator granted Michael his wish. Where any of Gabrielle's or his warriors, attendants, sacred seeds, and spiritual animals fell, the spirit of life would go back into the light of the heavens.

Michael bowed his head. "Thank you," he said.

Then he turned to his army. "Let's open this gate and move forward."

Sun-Star looked over at Michael. "Does that key even fit?"

Michael examined the gate. "Let's hope so."

He placed the key into the keyhole and the images came back to life. When Michael turned the key, the enormous gate opened. All that had been resting on it vanished behind a cloud of black smoke.

The bronze image of a man whom they believed might be a pharaoh stayed in its place. They all mounted their black stallions and rode on, wondering why it had stayed. Sun-Star's owl took flight, along with a raven and hawk. The majestic spirit animals roamed in the southern sky. The vision beyond the gate was of a massive landscape filled with blossoming trees and a lush forest that extended to the horizon. Winding paths stretched far beyond their view ahead. They saw snowcapped mountains, oceans, and flowing rivers and seas. Many types of unfamiliar animals ran past them; strange-looking birds flew by. The bronze gate's entrance had brought them to an additional part of the planet and the vision dazzled everyone. Michael could not believe his eyes. The planet's beauty was like nothing he had ever seen.

"I wonder, Father, those things that were on that bronze gate appear to have disappeared, except for the one man. Our planet is full of them, they scattered all over the place. It's just a thought, but should we be concerned about this?" Sun-Star shrugged his shoulders. He was worried about the mermaid who had captivated him. She now roams around on the new planet, and he knew he must be aware.

"We must remain vigilant, Sun-Star," Michael replied.

"Did you memorize what was on that mysterious gate?" Michael asked Dante.

"I did not, my lord. But I am sure that if we meet up with any of them, I will remember."

Efren slowed his stallion and turned toward Michael. "My lord, I am aware of what now lurks ahead of us."

"Efren, you never cease to amaze me," Michael said.

"Thank you, my lord."

"Ride on, my family. Straight ahead we go."

Sun-Star shifted in his saddle. "Look what's ahead, the Tree of Life," he said.

"Look at the Fountain of Enlightenment," Michael replied.

They dismounted and walked over to the Tree of Life. It was vibrant and alive. The fountain's rippling waters revealed another black clamshell. Michael picked it up, saw that it was unopened, and placed it in his satchel. This shell would reveal his next destination.

Efren walked alongside Michael and let him know he would move onward.

"My lord, on the horizon there appears to be a long house with a glowing object in front of it. I will ride ahead with our spirit animals to see what is before us."

"Okay," Michael replied. "Be safe. Sun-Star and I will wait under the Tree of Life until you return."

The flashing trails from a source of light had now crashed down on the west side of the new planet. A tremendous explosion shook the planet with violent intensity. Echoes of thunder rumbled through the sky. Michael believed the mighty forces were now approaching, and he was not sure where they were. Sun-Star became agitated with the noise that had fallen upon the planet.

"The storm is getting worse. That bang was so violent, it caused the planet to vibrate."

Michael turned and reassured Sun-Star. "I know. But just remember that we do not know what is ahead. We must always be prepared, and whatever difficulties we face, I am sure we are capable, and we will deal with them."

But would they? Michael thought to himself. That explosion was tremendous; it seemed to have come from a violent source of power. Michael wondered what he would face along his path. The sky was getting darker, and sparks flashed across it. As Michael and Sun-Star waited for Efren to return, they gazed upon the sky and the glorious landscape.

"Are you scared?" Michael wanted to know.

Sun-Star reached out to his father and tapped his shoulder. "No. I have you, who will be the greatest commander by the orders of the heavens. We have Sariel, Efren, and our spirit animals by our sides, as well as our brothers in arms. They are a supreme army and our companions."

"Thank you for having so much faith in me."

Sun-Star smiled. "You're welcome, Dad."

Chapter Twenty
A Mystifying Appearance

Gabrielle rode on with Moon-Star and her army of female soldiers; their attendants followed behind with their supplies. Gabrielle looked sensational on her horse; she felt strong, but she also understood her role as the leader of a superior army. Moon-Star wore decorated, glittering white armor. A brilliant silver jeweled sword enclosed in a scabbard at her side. They attached their silver shields to their backs.

Ahead, they saw a gleam on the horizon. "I believe we have reached our first destination," Saffron said. "It is a large silver gate with many illustrations on it. My lady, I will ride ahead with our spirit animals to make sure there is no danger."

"Okay, Saffron. Please be safe," Gabrielle said.

Bright-eyed, Gabrielle looked over at Moon-Star. "I suppose you are ready, my beautiful daughter."

"Yes, I am. This is so exciting," she replied.

Saffron called upon power from her spiritual magic to produce an all-important paranormal result. She approached the silver gate and raised both hands. A burst of energy flowed from her fingertips toward it. As she used her magic, she drew in a strong, mysterious force with both her hands. Saffron placed a silver pentagram on the silver gate. Her pentagram pushed out several dynamic lightning bolts and then burned with a silvery flame. The pentagram remained firm on the gate, sparking bolts and blazing. It would ward off any evil that might harm them as they approached the gate. Satisfied, Saffron returned with good news.

"My lady, the gate is ready to be opened. The images are safe."

Saffron removed a likeness of a moon-shaped disk off the gate and passed it on to Gabrielle. "This will open the gate," she said.

The glittering moon disk intrigued Gabrielle. "Thank you."

Gabrielle looked over at Saffron and noticed a shining object around her neck.

"That necklace you are wearing is interesting, Saffron." She leaned forward and inspected. "What a beautiful silver amulet. It is a pentacle. Funny, I didn't notice it earlier."

They reached the large silver gate and saw the pentagram Saffron had placed. Several bolts of lightning cast back and forth with a luminous silver flame.

The calm presence of this wondrous silver gate astonished Gabrielle. The images looked to be alive. Butterflies hovered over fairies, and stone braziers lit with a faint fire. Falcons were in flight; lions roamed on the gate. Cypress trees and flowering cacti decorated the bridges. Arches had climbing vines. The aroma of sweet-scented oils drifted their way. The gate had large pearls and glittering jewels encrusted on it, and the smell of burning sweet wood billowed smoke around them. There was an army of Anubis erected on stands, and in the distance, magnificent chariots, royal carriages, and grand ships drifted in a cloud of smoke. Next, they saw the face of a silver woman, blurry in appearance, with her eyes closed. An amulet was around her neck; a scepter was above her head. There were scarabs, and even an enormous white cobra was slithering on the gate. A cryptic pyramid stood alone and appeared to be a powerful source of energy. Hazy clouds surrounded an ancient castle. In the distance, they saw sparkling spears, bows, and arrows. There were dark images of black shields bearing an unknown emblem, but then it became visible. Three ghostly dragons were in flight, and as they turned their heads, they peered down at the travelers with their piercing, jeweled eyes.

Gabrielle felt a sense of uneasiness. She looked at Saffron and was a bit confused. "Saffron, what does this all mean?"

"Look toward the sky and you will see Hamuel—he will tell you."

A swirl of energy drifted in front of them, and the sun set down a solar flare and sparked a light. Hamuel now stood in front of the silver gate, and the gate became still. He who sees the Creator in the heavens then spoke to Gabrielle.

"Lady Gabrielle, I have the power to guide and protect you and your army. When I place my symbol beside Sariel's mark, your shields will become impenetrable. When I place a sword on all your shields, you may never need another. And I give you the strength not to fear what is ahead. The Divine has placed many seeds on this planet, some of them good and some of them are evil. You will know which one is which. Call upon your shield when you need a helping hand. My lady, you are nearing your oath." He bowed and vanished.

Gabrielle looked over to Saffron. Then she turned to Moon-Star. "Our fate is ahead, and so is my oath. Are you ready?"

With Saffron and her mother at her side, Moon-Star felt confident. "Oh, yes. I am prepared for this and so are our sisters in arms."

Gabrielle looked behind her and saw that her army was ready to fight. She turned her brilliant white horse to face them and raised her mighty sword. "You are all my family, sent to me from the heavens," she said in an authoritative voice. "I am your leader. I promise to protect you all as best as the spiritual world will allow me. You are a glorious gift sent to me. My new family, you will always be in my heart, as will be my brother who is on Earth."

Gabrielle could feel her emotions rising. "I am the Guardian of Moon-Star. We must all protect her, and she will be our queen."

Gabrielle's army raised their silver swords, and her attendants stood by and cheered along. "Hail to our mighty future queen, hail to the future queen's mother, Lady Gabrielle." The sound of cheering echoed in the proximity.

Gabrielle moved forward. The spirit birds were flying high in the sky above her and beyond the horizon. Gabrielle's spirit animals traveled alongside and with watchful eyes. Her army followed along with their attendants and supplies. Gabrielle dismounted her horse to open the gate; this would lead her to her destination. She placed the moon disk and turned it, which caused the silver gate to come alive with an active energy that was flowing like a river. Then everything that had been on the gate disappeared. Except for the silver image of a woman.

Gabrielle was confused. "That's strange, Saffron. This womanly image is still on this gate; why is that?"

"She looks to be royalty, my lady," Saffron replied. "She might be a queen. The heavens have not set her fate into place, so we need not worry. But I will keep her in mind."

"Thank you, Saffron," Gabrielle said and was ready to move on.

The massive silver gate opened. They observed two large obelisks with two images perched on the top of them. The one on the left was a sun, and the right one was a moon. Gabrielle realized that there was a Sun-Star.

"Come here, Moon-Star, I want you to see a luminary." Gabrielle beamed with a sudden realization. "Michael must have Sun-Star."

With a great deal of excitement, she pointed to the sun on top of the obelisk. She touched Moon-Star's hand. "Oh, I believe you are Sun-Star's destiny, and you are his."

Moon-Star was ecstatic. "This is so exciting." Her words poured. "To know that I have a Sun-Star as my destiny."

Moon-Star became dreamy again—she liked to do this. "What does he look like?" she asked Gabrielle. "Is he handsome like Michael?"

Gabrielle was about to tell Moon-Star, but Saffron winked at her. "Let me take care of this, my lady."

"The heavens say he is a handsome man, my future queen. He has a magical glow around him. He is tall, with broad shoulders, blond hair, and dazzling hazel eyes. And he is your destiny."

Gabrielle smiled. "He will be king, and you will be his queen."

She then pointed to the obelisk and showed Moon-Star the royal crowns placed under the sun and moon.

Then Moon-Star turned to Saffron. "You say he is bright and handsome. Oh, Saffron, Mother, I am falling in love."

Gabrielle burst out laughing. "Okay, my faraway girl, it's time to keep a focus on the journey for now. We will both have our destinies in our arms in time."

Moon-Star had entered a brand-new phase in her life. She knew she had a dream man to fight for, and she wanted to reach him.

Gabrielle signaled her army to move forward. As they rode along, the ground formed grassy trails, and snowcapped mountains were beyond. Cypress trees, fruit trees, and the meadows had fresh blossoming flowers. Birds flew over the horizon, and colorful butterflies drifted alongside them. They saw an endless river and a calm blue ocean. With her watchful eyes, Gabrielle inspected the surroundings. They reached the obelisk, which had many images upon it, and it drew their attention to an eye-catching view. Gabrielle saw 3-D cards.

"What cards are these, Saffron? What do you make of this?"

"My lady, these are spiritual cards from the Divine. There is a Queen of Wands. She is an educated woman associated with Sun-Star. Over here, we have the King of Wands. He is an educated man associated with Moon-Star," she said and winked at Moon-Star.

"And here we have the High Priestess. She is also a spiritual woman," Saffron concluded.

Sure enough, there was a magical appearance. The High Priestess, draped in glorious silks and embroidered satins, floated down and off the obelisk; her long blond hair carried a luster, and her green eyes were exquisite. She walked toward Gabrielle and greeted her. The 3-D cards on the obelisk flew down and went into the High Priestess's hands, then vanished.

The High Priestess bowed. "Hello, my future queen, my lady, and Saffron," she sent out a friendly greeting. "Welcome to your first destination. The 3-D images you see on the obelisk are spiritual cards. My cards will reveal what is ahead. I am your High Priestess," she said. "I might join you in your journeys; this I will know in time. For now, I look forward to reading the meanings of these magical cards."

Seeing a High Priestess astounded Gabrielle. "Thank you. I am most grateful. What do you think, Moon-Star?"

"Well, this is important," she replied. "We have Saffron, Hamuel, and Sariel on our shields, and the possibility of a High Priestess to watch over us," she said.

Saffron looked over at the beautiful High Priestess. "This is a wondrous time in our journey. We are fortunate to meet up with such a high-ranking woman," Saffron said and bowed her head to the High Priestess.

The High Priestess floated toward a path that led them to their first destination. She stopped and waved her hand to the right, and the Fountain of Enlightenment appeared. "Approach the fountain, my lady, and you will find your next clamshell," she said.

Gabrielle and Moon-Star dismounted from their beautiful horses and walked over to the fountain to find an unopened white clamshell. Gabrielle placed it in her satchel, and they both mounted their horses once again. They all continued to ride along a path that led to a large ancient castle. The High Priestess had rainbows of colors following her and butterflies were flitting all around her. Ivies climbed up trees as everything she passed came to life.

Moon-Star remained mystified by the view. "Oh, the splendid smell of those flowers and lavender; it is so fresh and invigorating. Look at the ponds. They even have floating water lilies with frogs and toads hopping along with them."

Gabrielle looked over at Saffron, and they both smiled. The land had transformed into a colorful landscape.

Gabrielle noticed on the horizon that the sky was streaked with a flame. Solar flares came packed with a high energy; this energy had been roaming around the planet all day without letting up. Gabrielle wondered why there was so much activity in the sky—she found this worrisome. While admiring their first destination, they approached a vast castle surrounded by a huge white cloud. Positioned out front were hundreds of lit torches, along with lit lanterns and flickering candles. Water flowed through the moat that encircled the castle. The drawbridge was down and guarded.

The High Priestess stopped. "You will all sleep here tonight and prepare for the journey ahead. We will feast and enjoy our evening, as we have much to talk about."

Saffron approached Gabrielle. "I will tend to the army, the attendants, and our spirit animals, to ensure that they get fed and rested. I will prepare them for our journey."

"Thank you, Saffron," Gabrielle said. "I don't know what we would do without you."

Saffron bowed her head. "Thank you, my lady."

Saffron rode off to the castle grounds and led the army, attendants, and animals to their resting places. The clouds rumbled with thunder and lightning brightened the sky. Everyone moved onto the castle grounds for safety. Gabrielle and Moon-Star waited at the front of the castle's entrance and noticed the Tree of Life was beside the castle. The spirit animals then assumed their positions at their side, guarding them.

Gabrielle looked to the horizon and saw streams of light heading down and striking the west side of the new planet. Then there was a tremendous sound, and it vibrated the ground. Flashes of lightning struck the ground, while sounds of thunder rumbled through the sky. This startled Moon-Star and Gabrielle.

Gabrielle wondered about this additional force and what it meant for the planet. Her senses heightened, and she understood to a certain extent it happened on the west side. She believed this was not good. The castle gates closed.

Chapter Twenty-One
Visions of a Burning Flame

Michael looked at Sun-Star in surprise. "You called me 'Dad.'"

"Yes, Dad. Efren mentioned for my age, I should call you Dad. Efren also said that saying Father is still okay, but I like Dad."

"Efren is right, and it feels good to be a dad, especially to a future king," Michael said.

Content and watching his surroundings, Sun-Star spotted Efren. "Dad, here comes Efren and our spirit animals."

Sun-Star's owl was in flight; their raven and hawk were soaring high in the sky. Efren rode up the path with the spirit animals.

Efren looked excited. "I bring good news, my lord. As I passed through the countryside, I found a town. Two large rivers, a large forest, and a dark sea surround it, and it is just ahead of us. In fact, there are people awaiting your arrival."

"Splendid," Michael said. "Well, we should move ahead. We don't want to waste any time."

Efren turned to the army, attendants, and spirit animals. "Move forward," he said and waved his arm to point the way.

They heard a crashing noise. Thunder and lightning ripped through the open sky as a solar storm erupted. Michael looked up at it, worried. They approached the quaint small town to see a long house. An image beyond appeared to be an inferno that glowed with intensity. They arrived in the town, dismounted, and handed the reins to their attendants.

Efren assessed the area. "My lord, this is your first stop. I will tend to the army, attendants, and spirit animals. If there is anything you need, please let me know."

"Thank you. But please stay close. You know you are carrying precious cargo."

"What would that be?" Efren inquired.

Michael leaned over. "I am speaking of my wine," he said, and winked.

Efren laughed. "I will guard your wine with my life, my lord."

"I know you will. You enjoy it as well," Michael said.

Efren went on with the army, the attendants, and their sacred native spirit animals to rest in the town. Michael and Sun-Star walked toward the house. A beautiful lady with long, dark hair greeted the men. They both noticed her lovely green eyes. She had a white cloak draped over her shoulders.

"Hello, my future king and my lord. We have been waiting for you. We will have a grand feast once you have both settled in. Please come this way."

Upon entering, they noticed a large family wearing white cloaks standing behind a long table, covered in crafted embroidered linen. There was a distinct scent of burning incense, and flickering candles cast shadows across the walls. A tall man dressed in a white robe met Lord Michael and the future King Sun-Star.

"Welcome, my lord. I am Paul." He bowed his head, then the rest also bowed their heads.

"Praise to our mighty future king, praise to the future kings father, Lord Michael," the crowd said as one.

"I will be one of your mentors." Paul directed them to the table where two high-backed chairs were in waiting.

"Sit, please. We will feast and celebrate your arrival in this glorious kingdom," Paul said.

Michael and Sun-Star were both amazed to see such a radiant family inside this vast house. The heavens had put down this spectacular house in the earlier stages of the planet's creation in secrecy. The heavens selected Paul and his family of brothers and sisters to be a leading light to aid Michael and Sun-Star on their journey.

Paul turned to them. "Here is where you will begin your journey. I will set the prophecies into place. This is where you will determine how to secure the survival of the King Sun-Star and Queen Moon-Star. Beyond this house, there is a sacred tent which you and Sun-Star must enter. We will explain in time. For now, let us eat lamb and bread and drink wine."

Michael looked around and saw two decanters, one containing white wine and the other red wine. He also saw gold chalices at the end of the table. His eyes lit up. "I would love to have a drink of wine."

Sun-Star laughed. "Me too," he said with a wide grin on his face.

Sun-Star walked over to the table and mingled with the crowd. He took a chalice full of white wine. Then he swirled his wine so that it touched the brim of his chalice and sniffed it. Michael watched him and chuckled.

Michael went to join him. "Give me one of those chalices, please," he said. Sun-Star regarded his dad and handed him a chalice of red wine.

Paul's family prepared for them a feast, and at the end, Michael placed his hand out to shake Paul's. "Thank you for the delicious meal and the wine."

"You're welcome, my lord. Let me show you to your rooms." They headed to their rooms and had a good night's sleep.

***

Morning arrived, and Michael went out of the house to go check on Efren. He noticed the preparations for the next leg of their journey. Spirit animals were sitting by the carriages and the attendants were loading them with supplies. The army was tending to the horses.

"Nice job, Efren," he said. "I will return later with Sun-Star; he's still sleeping."

"Too much wine last night, my lord," Efren said.

"Sun-Star's been drinking it like water. We're going to keep a close eye on him."

They both doubled over with laughter.

"We will continue to prepare for our journey until then, my lord," Efren said.

"And we'll stay away from the wine." They both chuckled.

Michael patted his stallion on the head. Efren and the spirit animals watched him walk toward the house, to wake Sun-Star up. Sariel, the supreme commander of the great council, and Dante the Fool had shown up, and they were all waiting.

Michael entered the house and saw Sun-Star was naked. "What is this?" he said in a bewildered tone.

"Please remove your clothing," Paul asked him. "You both need to bathe in these scented oils. We must prepare you to be received in the sacred tent."

Michael did not ask questions. There was a large body of water rippling ahead and burning braziers surrounding the area. A light gust of wind was blowing the silk curtains from side to side. As he undressed, Michael glanced over at Sun-Star, and they walked toward the water. They slipped in and bathed, and the aroma of incense was thick in the air. A sense of serenity fell upon them both. Michael lay back and felt at ease. As they stepped out of the spiraling water, they draped towels over them. Paul moved toward them, with clothing draped over his arm. Soon, Michael and Sun-Star dressed in blue embroidered ephods. A servant carried in jeweled breastplates and placed them over their chests. Gold chains attached the sides to each other, and a king's crown stamped itself on each left corner. Their magnificent bronze swords settled by their sides; their bronze shields were in their hands. They looked at each other in admiration.

Paul approached Michael and Sun-Star.

"This is your day of reward, and you will take an oath, Lord Michael. I will bring you to the divine tent, where you will be in spiritual harmony with the Creator. You have fasted this day and washed your hands and feet in sacred water. I will anoint you with heavenly blood and oil."

He guided them to a large tent. What they had seen during the night as dynamic, luminous flames now appeared as a white cloud encompassing the tent.

Sun-Star watched his father.

Michael stopped and turned his head; he could hear a soft voice whispering.

"Move over to stand upon this rock."

Michael did so and a misty cloud floated toward him, then a blurred figure of a man in a white robe came into view. The faint image brushed up alongside him, raising his arm. Michael felt remarkable energy flowing through his body, then he could see this ethereal man in his vision. Michael bowed his head in silence. This was an extraordinary meeting, and Michael would never forget it.

Eleven men and their sisters approached the tent, and Paul conferred with them.

"You are ready to enter the sacred tent. Bring these burnt offerings and place them on the table along with this bread and wine. You are the selected star seeds; you must be pure. This is where Sun-Star will secure his title as king," Paul said.

Paul bowed his head. "You are now ready to receive the Divine Spirit. Please follow me."

A flash of light appeared in front of them. Paul opened the ram skin curtain, and they all moved forward. Inside, on the north side, they saw a table covered with a decorative embroidered cloth and bronze stands with burning lamps filled with olive oil. They placed the offerings on the table and bowed their heads. Michael and Sun-Star both walked back to see another decorated table on the south side. There, two sparkling crystal amethyst jewels and a gold papyrus sheet with silver writing were on the table.

They read: Infuse these precious stones into your swords.

Michael and Sun-Star took the brilliant crystal amethysts and scraped them along their sword's edge. The swords sparked and lit up. The infused amethysts had transformed them into radiant swords, with the amethysts bordered on the edge of their grips. On the east side, a papyrus sheet appeared and directed them to put the silver box he had picked up earlier on the table. When Michael did so, a pouch containing coins came into view and he took them and placed them in his satchel. Michael and Sun-Star looked toward the west, to see writing on papyrus that instructed them to place their shields on the west wall, which they did. Lightning bolts flashed and struck their shields, and these embedded a symbol of justice into their shields alongside Sariel's symbol. A luminous sword became apparent on their shields, and they both acknowledged it filled these swords with limitless power.

"The pentacle is a spiritual gift on your shields," Paul said. "It is the fifth element, and it will charge your shields. The power of the heavens is on these shields, and anyone from the dark side who touches them will die. Wave your arm over the east side of the wall."

Michael waved his arm, and what it revealed to him were golden bows with shimmering quivers, diamond-tipped arrows, and alongside them, glittering, sequined spears. He saw suits of magical dark armor and crafted whips, axes, knives, daggers, and shackles. Stored nearby hung embroidered garments, leather satchels, and long, black-hooded cloaks bearing a sacred emblem.

"These are your gifts from the heavens," Paul said.

Paul read the final golden papyrus. The quill swirled with silver writing and brought to light a heavenly message:

You have given me burnt offerings, bread, and wine. Your fellowship and oath to the heavens are now complete. Lord Michael and King Sun-Star anoint each other with the sacred blood and oil from the gilded chalice.

They both felt serene, and a mass of white clouds floated around them.

"You are now consecrated," a powerful voice spoke.

"Place your clamshell upon the table. I will write about your journey for you," Paul said.

The black shell flickered, then opened. The last message revealed itself.

"This tent will travel with you on your journeys; you will collect sacred items to be placed in here."

Paul raised his arms. "Lord Michael and King Sun-Star, study your surroundings. This thought process gives you time to prepare yourself for your next destination, and this will come soon."

Michael and Sun-Star bowed their heads, knowing that they stood by the Creator. They were to spend seven days in the tent. Efren, the sacred native spirit animals, Dante, the attendants, Michael's army, and Sariel, the commander and leader, waited outside, guarding the heavenly tent, and awaited Michael's command. The attendants continued to organize for the next leg of their journey.

Chapter Twenty-Two
Escorted by the High Priestess

Saffron returned and saw Gabrielle and Moon-Star were still on the castle grounds. They dismounted their horses when they saw her. Saffron fetched Moon-Star and Gabrielle's horses. Gabrielle turned toward Saffron, and said, "We must have an enjoyable time this evening," and smiled. "Moon-Star and I were just browsing around the place. It's magnificent here, but a storm is brewing over there."

As Gabrielle and Moon-Star entered the castle, trumpets announced their arrival. The High Priestess walked up and introduced Gabrielle and Moon-Star to a woman and man who had been waiting for their arrival. She was a tall, blonde woman dressed in a long white wizard's cloak embroidered with magical images that were bursting with color. "This is Valda," the High Priestess said.

Gabrielle and Moon-Star looked at the couple. "Hello, nice to meet you, Valda," Gabrielle said.

"Nice to meet you, Valda," Moon-Star echoed.

Next, the High Priestess turned to a tall, brown-haired man wearing a long black wizard's cloak embroidered with mystical images. "This is Vance."

Gabrielle smiled. "Hello, Vance. Nice to meet you."

Moon-Star greeted him too.

Valda and Vance bowed to Gabrielle and Moon-Star.

The High Priestess then announced, "Good news, my lady. The prophecy states Valda and Vance will marry the king and queen."

Moon-Star glanced over at Gabrielle. "Oh, my fabulous wedding. This will be a wonderful day. But I have not met my king yet, so this wedding won't be soon enough for me. But to have two wizards performing the ceremony is an honor." She was once again in a dream world.

Gabrielle agreed. "Yes, when the time comes, it will be an imperial celebration."

Gabrielle turned to the couple. "Please don't pay any attention to Moon-Star. She is my faraway girl, dreaming of her king in shining armor. We all have something to look forward to."

They all looked over at Moon-Star and smiled. Then the High Priestess turned back to Gabrielle. "Valda and Vance understand a special book you brought on your journey. This is the book you took off the Golden Door. It has buried enigmas and knowledge for a secretive magic only used by wizards. The Creator positioned a glorious castle on this planet when it was in its final formation, along with wizards, Valda, and Vance. They are here to be of service to you, my lady."

"That is wonderful, thank you. I will give them the book," Gabrielle said.

Gabrielle reached into her satchel and knew this book belonged to an important person. She was the deliverer and handed it to Valda, who bowed her head.

"This book holds the secrets of wizardry and the locations of the portals to Earth. It will be safe in our hands and guarded by the great white dragon and black cobra. This book is now for our eyes only."

In return, Vance handed Gabrielle a sealed golden box. "Carry this with you, my lady. This shimmering box will unleash a special power from the heavens. Valda and I do not know what kind of power this is. But what I know is you will need it during your journey. When that time arrives, you will be familiar with its force."

The glittering box excited Gabrielle: she noticed unusual imagery etched on its outer surface. She put the small box in her satchel and said, "Thank you for this glorious gift."

"Well, now that is all settled," Vance said. "Would you like to have a bit of fun with us?"

Gabrielle and Moon-Star both smiled.

"Can you tell me who is yin and who is yang?" The wizards flared their cloaks around.

They laughed. "We don't know," Gabrielle said. "But maybe because you're wearing black, you are yin. And Valda, you're wearing white, so you must be yang."

They all cheered. "Hurrah. Lady Gabrielle got it," Valda said.

"Okay, now that I figured that out, can you please explain?" Gabrielle asked.

"Come into the castle. We will get you settled in."

The attendants brought Gabrielle and Moon-Star each a drink and a tray filled with a variety of fruit.

They sat, and Valda and Vance explained the secrets of yin and yang.

"I am the yin of the book of magic and the spells of the dark side," Vance said. "My celestial power can ward off the evil that may come into our path and lead to yours."

"I am the yang, which enables me to see the bright side of the book,". Valda said. She would control a portal to Earth.

"We balance this book, Lady Gabrielle. Our celestial powers can control the good and evil," Vance said.

Valda and Vance's yin and yang reversed, a key mystery they knew nothing of. Valda held the bright side of the male energy yang; Vance held the dark side of the female energy yin.

Gabrielle acknowledged them both. "Thank you both for explaining all of this. Everything seems so complicated, and there is so much to know." She turned and took in her surroundings. "Your castle is impressive; the craftsmanship and beauty are exquisite."

"You can relax and bathe. This evening there will be a glorious feast to celebrate your arrival," the High Priestess mentioned.

The attendants escorted Gabrielle and Moon-Star to their rooms. Lanterns cast shadows on the castle walls and brightened the room. The large, draped silk curtains on the acacia windows swayed in the light breeze. An aromatic oil burned with the aroma of flowers, and it came their way. Attendants drew a bath for them. Jasmine flowers floated on the oil-infused water. The view out the window was a brilliant landscape adorned with magnificent trees.

Moon-Star stayed captivated. "This castle is beautiful."

"Yes, this place is breathtaking. Now let's get bathed and rested," Gabrielle agreed.

After they rested, Gabrielle and Moon-Star entered a grand room, wearing clothing crafted for them by the wizards, which comprised beautiful embroidered silk dresses and leather sandals. Their hair looked braided and decorated with daisies. Gabrielle smiled when she saw her family, who had arranged the gala, all seated at a long table laden with food and adorned with flowers. Musicians ran their fingers over harp strings, and dancers wearing colorful satin gowns were gliding across the floor. Their floating silk scarves fascinated Gabrielle. Attendants entered the banquet hall, carrying trays laden with roast lamb, baby calves, stuffed pigs, pheasant breasts, fruit, vegetables, bread, and wine. Gabrielle looked over at Saffron, the spirit animals, her attendants, and her glorious army. They were all present and sitting on both sides of the table. They were enjoying the festivities. It was an enormous castle, and in the far corner on the floor were large troughs. Inside the troughs was a spiraling of cosmic energy for the spirit animals to feast on.

Moon-Star was in her glory. "This is fabulous. Look at all this food." Her eyes were bright with anticipation of the upcoming feast.

Gabrielle took a seat beside the High Priestess and motioned to Moon-Star to join them. "Shall we? This looks fabulous."

"I've never seen such food! It's like a dream," Moon-Star said.

Gabrielle laughed. "Yes, it is. Enjoy."

As the evening progressed, the High Priestess leaned toward Gabrielle. "My lady, after dinner, we will take tea into the grand library. Valda, Vance, Saffron, and Hamuel will be present."

"This is wonderful news," Gabrielle said. "We look forward to it. How does that sound to you, Moon-Star?"

Moon-Star giggled. "Will there be any dessert?"

"Yes, my future queen, there will be dessert." Valda could not contain his laughter.

Moon-Star's eyes lit up. "Oh, great. My mother told me about this delicious part of a meal. I have been dreaming of a tantalizing piece of warm bread or even chocolate chip cookies or a cake topped with icing."

Gabrielle leaned toward Moon-Star. "Me too," she said and laughed. "I told you about my cooking on Earth, and the delicious desserts I have made. I enjoy doing this very much, and I can see you now have an interest too. Cooking and baking are two of my passions."

Moon-Star grabbed Gabrielle's hand as they entered the luxurious library. Gabrielle saw Saffron approaching.

"My lady, I set all into place the attendants, your army, and the spirit animals. We can depart first thing in the morning."

The library was a masterpiece crafted in acacia woodwork, and the pictured view was the spectacular countryside. Before them was a large marble table, covered in fine embroidered linen. The moon-and-sun centerpiece had every type of pastry imaginable. Moon-Star licked her lips. They all sat and enjoyed a cup of tea and desserts.

"Welcome again, my lady and my future queen," the High Priestess said. "Can you please bring out the royal scepters?"

Gabrielle reached into her satchel and pulled out two glittering scepters. They all looked toward an open window where they saw an astral flare shooting across the landscape. The winds carried in a luminous flame of many colors. In the distance, a woman of great beauty emerged from the flame. She crossed the landscape, entered the castle grounds, and drifted into the room.

The Queen of Scepters was a vision to behold. She had curly black hair, huge blue eyes that glittered like stars, and she was wearing a glamorous purple gown. When Gabrielle handed her the scepters, she held them up in the air and performed with a spellbinding, swirling motion. "It is now set into place," she said. "These scepters have magical powers. Carry them on your wedding day, future queen Moon-Star. You and your future King Sun-Star will be the rulers of the new planet; this is your world, and you will rule it with your soon-to-be king."

"Thank you, Queen of Scepters," Moon-Star said. "I hope you can join us when I get married to the man I am destined for."

"I will be there; this will be such an honor for me," the Queen of Scepters said and bowed.

The High Priestess disappeared for a brief time and reappeared again. She walked toward Gabrielle. "My lady, Hamuel and Sariel have clearance from the Creator, I may join you on your journey."

"This is wonderful news!" Gabrielle said.

The High Priestess directed Gabrielle and Moon-Star to a different table. "Now, please, come and sit over here."

Gabrielle looked at the two high-backed wooden chairs with lion paws on their armrests and their feet. The seats were red velvet. A round marble table displayed embroidered white linen.

The High Priestess sat. "I will read the hidden images that were placed on the obelisk," she said. "I will tell you what they mean for both you and Moon-Star."

The smell of incense lingered, and candles lit the ceiling in all directions. Scented wood was burning in the stone fireplace, and the aroma put them at ease. Gabrielle and the Moon-Star felt content and relaxed sitting by the High Priestess.

"Let me tell you a little about myself. I am the Creator's (II) the High Priestess in the divine cards, there is no other. In one hand is my crystal ball; my spirited book and divine cards remain in the other. I am an expert on the internal world and outer space. My spiritual powers can foresee matters not yet revealed, and my inner illumination brings moral guidance. When I look within for the hidden messages in dreams, my esoteric knowledge and wisdom pull them into my view. I see invisible aspects of the universe where I can unlock mysteries and reveal secrets of the unknown. I am the celestial Mother."

Seventy-eight spiritual cards went up in the air; sparks of lightning flashed a fire to surround them. The cards floated in midair, and then the deck revealed a card. All remaining cards vanished. The first card fell into the High Priestess's hand, and she pulled it toward her heart. According to the High Priestess, the cards floated above her head.

"The first card is the Queen of Wands. This is Moon-Star, our queen. The sun shines on your heart. You will sit on your throne with the sun symbol, and by your side will be a lion of fire and strength. You are full of fiery energy, and your desire for your king has heightened. Your inner fire is burning, which means the possibilities for you are endless. You will accept your leadership and become a commanding warrior with a tireless passion. Look beyond the surface for your light, have faith in your instincts, and remember to value your worth. Embrace who you are, reach beyond the stars. You are the Moon-Star. Your connection to the cosmos is at an imperial level. You are a heavenly star seed birthed by the heavens, the true ruler of the new planet. You have the power of positive thinking and good advice to offer. The knowledge you carry is from the Creator. Warmth and love surround you, and courage and passion will always be with you. You are an attractive, magnetic, mature woman now.

"The second card is the King of Wands. This man is Sun-Star, our king, a man of authority and strength. His strengths are devotion to his cause, and he has strong leadership. He sits upon a throne, and a moon symbol sits alongside him. The magic of the moon will brighten his heart, and he will be tireless in his passion for his queen. The king will have the strength and knowledge to battle in warfare. He will fight until death to reign as king of the new planet. Sun-Star is an ambitious man. He has learned patience and power. Sun-Star is a brilliant man who is skilled and committed to his purpose. He has the talents he needs to rule the new planet. King Sun-Star has positive energy, and it flows like the mighty rivers. You are his destiny, my Queen. Sun-Star yearns for your love and affection. He awaits you.

"The third card is the Lover Card. This is a good start, Lady Gabrielle, and I will now speak of Michael. You have both had an extended period of waiting to get beyond this point in your journey. You both have put in sincere efforts and have faith in your future. This is a joint creative endeavor. It involves both personal growth and intuition. The preparation for this journey has led you both to succeed. Lady Gabrielle, you and Lord Michael remain enchanted with the love for each other. You are both heading in the right direction, but you are still in the initial stages of your journeys. Now it is time to deal with any problems. Lord Michael and you can achieve your goals if you stay on the same path and go according to plan.

"The fourth card is blank, but it represents the new world. This futuristic planet awaits its king and queen. It is a brand-new beginning with new promises brought upon us by the heavens. It brings a better life, with peace, love, happiness, and joy, and where success and victory are in the future. There are four corners, four seasons, and four elements. Your inner spirits will bring you to deep understandings in many situations. This journey will have major life cycles and hardships, and emotions will all be a factor. One part of this planet bears a dark side, and the time will come to stake your claim. This is the promised kingdom with expanded horizons, and you must reach the end. Take this world into your hands, Lady Gabrielle, along with Lord Michael, and hang on to it. No matter what happens, believe and the magic will happen. It will come from a cosmic flow. You have a special life, with spiritual beginnings. This is the end of a phase and the start of a new one.

"The fifth card is also blank, but it represents a focus. You have a great parent-child relationship. Your Moon-Star has grown into a brilliant and beautiful woman. Both of you united with a trust, and will have emotional completion, but also protection, love, and contentment. An extraordinary happiness with the realization that a destiny lies ahead for you both. This is a positive card for matters of love and harmonious relationships. The heavens have bestowed a spiritual journey upon you, Lady Gabrielle, and on my queen. Now you both need to stop for a moment and appreciate all that has come your way. Be grateful, as the blessings will keep coming. Follow your hearts, my Queen, and my lady.

"The sixth card is blank too, but represents the difficulties of your journey. Rapid change is on the upside of a cycle. Both fate and progress are in your destiny. These are important developments. Unusual doors will open, and you will get timely breaks. This card foretells the end of one phase and the starting of a new one. Also, games of chance and lady luck are on your side. You are now entering an advanced cycle. You may have to make a crucial decision that will influence the unfolding of an event in your life. A different chapter in your life is about to begin, and there will be negative external forces around. Your karma will step in and take its place. You will have a radiant energy in your heart. Things will happen in cycles. You can face adversity and conquer it. The universe has great affirmations ahead for you, Lady Gabrielle. They will flow toward you. Stay positive, as this cycle will transform.

"The seventh card is me—II the High Priestess. I am your celestial light, Lady Gabrielle. I carry your higher power and can hear your inner voice. It will be me guiding you. The symbol of knowledge is on me. I am the goddess that is associated with your moon and your Moon-Star. The guardian of your subconscious is me. I will guide and protect you. Always look to me for guidance when you are in need. But there are dark seeds planted on this new planet of which I do not know. This is where I will try to guide where possible. You need to stay focused and make me aware if your celestial light becomes distorted, so I can plant my seeds of protection in your path."

Gabrielle glanced over at Moon-Star and noted her enlightenment. The High Priestess had uplifted and enlightened them both, and they were thankful for her insights.

"We both understand what is ahead of us, High Priestess. I am so thankful you have made me aware of everything that is to come—both the good and the bad. I am comforted by your faith in me, and I will use all my celestial strength to conquer evil."

"Just know, my lady," the High Priestess replied. "Your outcome could be quite favorable. As of now, Moon-Star is your top priority, we must crown her queen. You must reach your last destination. We will all battle the darkness together. The celestial connections have given you, Moon-Star, and Saffron, the power of three. Saffron, our future queen, and you will form one of the greatest forces when it is time, and all will recognize it."

Gabrielle had a strange feeling, and the High Priestess sensed it too. She touched Gabrielle's hand and got a vibrating signal. By fair means or foul, the High Priestess stayed blocked, and she could not get into Gabrielle's thoughts to see what it was. She pulled her hand away and was now aware it would happen on Gabrielle's journey, but that this vision reflected no danger to Gabrielle. This was a distant feeling of a dark secret, hidden in the back of her mind. The High Priestess wanted to know what it was, and she would keep this in mind and watch for any signs.

The High Priestess then rose, and she bowed. "Tomorrow afternoon is your day of reward, my lady. You will take an oath, and Moon-Star will secure her title as queen. You will both fast, bathe in scented oils, and dress in silks and satins so the Creator can receive you."

"Thank you for all being present," Gabrielle said.

Saffron got up and had a big smile on her face; Gabrielle sent her a wink.

Leaving the grand library, Gabrielle and Moon-Star walked through the long corridors that led them to their room. "The High Priestess has imparted such valuable information. I am thankful to have her with us."

"Yes, we are. But there is a perception about her I can't quite figure out. I guess I will learn more about her in time."

***

Morning arrived, and the attendants arrived to prepare Gabrielle and Moon-Star for their day of reward. They bathed in scented oils and white lilies floated in the rippling bathing water. Incense lingered, a spice flavor in the air; it carried a sense of warmth and peace. The attendants helped Gabrielle and Moon-Star dress in silks, satins, and leather sandals. They entwined daisies and laurels in their beautiful long, dark hair. The attendants placed breastplates with stamped impressions of a queen on the right side on them and draped them in jewels and gold chains. They fixed their silver swords at their sides, and they had their silver shields in their hands. They both stood by the window and gazed at the mystifying new planet as they waited for the High Priestess.

The High Priestess approached them, reaching out with both hands. "Come, your enlightenment with the Creator awaits."

They walked down a path that led to an archway covered in vines. Blooming flowers and an odor of lavender surrounded them. Gabrielle and Moon-Star walked to a garden where brilliant braziers were burning. They could see a large white cloud floating ahead, shadowing the ground.

"You are ready to enter the sacred garden. Bring these burnt offerings and place them on the table along with this bread and wine. You are the selected star seeds; you must be pure," the High Priestess said and went back to the castle. Gabrielle and Moon-Star took the gifts and walked into the garden and would remain there for seven days. Saffron, the High Priestess, Gabrielle's glorious army, the sacred native spirit animals, her attendants, and Raguelle remained outside of the sacred garden to guard and wait for her command.

"Moon-Star, bow your head, please. We are in the company of greatness."

"Yes, Mother."

To be continued...

About the Author

Sylvie is a writer of fiction and an accomplished photographer. The Guardians of the Sun-Star and Moon-Star is her first novel in a series. If you enjoy a fantasy book with layers of romance and astronomy, then continue the journey with Sylvie in Book II.

A Halloween Adventure with Jack and Ony Lantern is her most recently published book and her first children's book.